Vannatta, Dennis
This Time, This Place

DATE DUE

AUG 0 6 1998			
APR 11 '99			
DISCARD			

DEMCO

THIS TIME, THIS PLACE

THIS TIME, THIS PLACE

STORIES BY
DENNIS VANNATTA

WHITE PINE PRESS

ACKNOWLEDGEMENTS:

"Thetis, Mary, and Mother" previously appeared in slightly
different form in *The Quarterly;* "Beloved Juggler" in *The Antioch
Review;* "Chicken in the Barn" in *Sonora Review;* "The Wrong Time"
in *Sequoia;* "The *David* of Michelanelo" in *The Quarterly* and *The
Pushcart Prize XV;* "Rumplestiltskin" in *Colorado-North Review;*
"Sometimes I Wonder" in *Sonoma Mandala;* "I in Renoir's
La Balancoire" in *Lullwater Review.*

Cover painting: *La Balançoire,* 1876. Pierre-Auguste Renoir. Used
by gracious permission of Musée d'Orsay, Paris.

Publication of this book was made possible, in part,
by grants from the
National Endowment for the Arts
and the
New York State Council on the Arts.

Printed in the United States of America

Book design by Watershed Design

ISBN 0-877727-01-6

WHITE PINE PRESS
76 Center Street
Fredonia, New York 14063

CONTENTS

for my father

THIS TIME, THIS PLACE

BELOVED JUGGLER

"Well, here goes. Let's just hope we don't get them both stuck up there," my dad said, rearing back with the football and taking dead aim at the whiffle ball I'd hit up into the maple tree, where it'd caught on the tip of a branch hanging out over the garden.

I was six or seven then—almost thirty years ago—but I can still see that football sailing up in a perfect spiral—I'd never seen anyone throw such a pass!—and hitting the whiffle ball dead center.

"Wow! Hot dog!" my dad laughed. I think he was more impressed than I was.

I rescued the ball from the tangle of dead tomato vines, and we walked back toward the house.

"Daddy, could you juggle both of these?" I asked, for no particular reason.

He eyed the balls a moment, then shrugged.

"Sure," he said, then without even glancing in that direction, pointed to the cord of wood stacked by the west fence, "and three of those logs."

"You could juggle these two balls and *three* of those logs?" I asked. I wanted to make sure I had this right.

"Sure. . .and that garbage can lid."

"*And* the garbage can lid?"

"Sure."

I was amazed.

"*Do* it, Daddy!"

"No, not now. I've already spent half-an-hour playing ball with you. I have work to do now."

"Naw, you couldn't really juggle all those," I decided. (I was slow, but not totally stupid.)

"Sure I could. Next time we play, remind me."

We were on the back porch. I pointed to the cardboard box filled with rusty springs that had sat in the corner of the porch for as long as I could remember. I never did know what the springs were for.

"Could you juggle that box of springs?"

"Do you mean with all the other stuff?—the balls and wood and stuff?"

"Yes, all of it."

"I could if you took the springs out of the box so I could juggle each of the springs separately. It'd be tough to do it with the springs in the box—tough, but not impossible."

"You couldn't do it."

"Yes I could. Next time we play, remind me."

We went on into the house.

"Could you juggle the trash can?"

"That'd be easy."

"Filled with garbage and trash and stuff?"

"Even easier. A little weight makes it easier to control."

"Daddy, you could not."

"Sure I could. And one of those kitchen chairs, the butcher knife, salt and pepper shakers, your mother's African violet,"—I followed him into the living room—"the newspaper, the magazine rack—"

"—Could you juggle the television?"

"No, not with the lead-ins attached, but I could juggle the TV stand and the platform rocker."

We went up the stairs.

"Daddy, could you juggle the *car?* Could you?"

"I don't like to brag, but yes, yes I could."

Mother was folding laundry on her and Dad's bed.

"And I could juggle the bedspread, both pillows, the window curtains, the chest-of-drawers—drawers in or out, your choice."

"Do you think you could help fold some of this laundry?" my mother asked.

He shook his head sadly.

"No, I'm only mortal, you know."

* * *

I remember pestering him for days afterward to juggle for me. He never did, of course—he always found some excuse not to—

but he never failed to tell me what he could and would juggle when the time was right.

Eventually I stopped asking him every day. (I seem to recall my mother throwing up her hands and exclaiming, "Paul, that's enough," but perhaps that's not how it ended.) I'd still ask him every once in awhile, though—maybe when getting out the football reminded me of it, for instance.

The years passed, and I became a sullen teenager. Once when I was in an especially foul mood, he tried to make me laugh by telling me how much he could juggle. I turned my back on him and walked out of the room, leaving him with his ottomans, string beans, and reams of typewriter paper spinning in the air.

Somehow, I evolved into a fully grown human being. I married, moved to a different state, fathered a son of my own. We'd visit my parents two or three times a year. My son would laugh indiscriminately at Pee-wee Herman and Freddie Kruger, but not at my father's juggling. I couldn't laugh either as I watched his right arm—stunned by his first stroke—manage only a spasm as he explained how he'd juggle this and that, this and that.

"He doesn't seem to get the joke, Dad," I apologized.

"Guess you had to be there," he shrugged.

"Had to be where?" my son asked.

My father and I knew, but we kept it to ourselves.

*   *   *

The second stroke finished him. By the time I'd flown in from New York, it was almost over. He lay stretched out on the hospital bed, hands flat at his sides, one tube up his left nostril, another hooked into the corner of his mouth. His eyes were slightly opened: sightless yellow slits.

Too numb for sorrow, I sat by his side for an hour, staring.

I took a tissue out of a little packet that was on the tray beside the bed and cleaned my glasses, then fiddled with the packet.

Without thinking about it and not even looking at my father I whispered, "Dad, could you juggle this?"

"Sure."

I started. I'd just imagined it, of course; yet there did seem to be something a little different about his eyes, a sort of *gathering,* a *clarification,* somehow.

I stood up and leaned over the bed and held the packet a few inches from his face.

"Dad, could you juggle this?" I asked again, smiling at my own foolishness.

"Sure."

I couldn't believe it. But, yes, this time he had, unquestionably, made a sound. Perhaps he hadn't really said "Sure," but some sort of liquid, sibilant sound had gurgled its way past the tube that, until that moment, seemed more alive than he. In fact, his lips, quite unmistakably, were trembling in a great effort to say something. I leaned down, my ear against his lips.

"Hand," he said.

"Hand?"

I looked at my hands first, then his. His right hand, which I could have sworn had been palm down on the bed, was now palm up. The middle finger was twitching.

For a moment I was at a loss; then it dawned on me.

"Oh, you want me to put the tissues in your hand?"

"Yes."

I laid the packet of tissues on his opened palm, and immediately his middle finger and thumb closed over it. I was dumbfounded, ready to ring for the nurse when I noticed that my father's eyes—no longer yellowish-red slits—were open, seeing, swinging to the right to look at me, I supposed, but no, he was searching the tray by his bed.

"Glasses," he said.

My mother had brought his glasses and placed them on the tray in their vinyl and velvet case.

"You want your glasses?"

"Hand."

I had it figured out now. I started to lay the glasses in his left hand, which was now palm up beside him. Then I hesitated.

"In the case, or out?"

"Your choice."

I placed them, in their case, in his palm.

"So," I said laughing, tears running down my cheeks, "you think you can juggle these tissues and your glasses?"

"Sure."

And, before I had a chance to reply, the box of tissues

somehow—I didn't even see his hand move—flipped in an arc over his body, just missing a collision with the glasses, which went sailing past, heading for his right hand.

"Dad!"

"Water glass," he said.

"What?"

"Water glass! Water glass!" he shouted impatiently, as if I were a little boy again and willfully disobeying him.

I took the water glass off the tray and then stood hesitantly by the bed. Before I could decide what to do, though, he had snatched it out of my hand and sent it into orbit with the tissues and glasses.

"Dad! You're OK! You're going to live!"

"Pitcher!" he ordered, ignoring what I thought was a fairly major issue.

But then, taking the pitcher in hand and trying to decide whether to dump the water before tossing it to him, I suddenly saw his point. What did anything else matter? He was, by God, *juggling!*

I tossed the pitcher, water and all, into the swirling triumvirate. He didn't bat an eye—caught it and sent it up.

By now he was sitting up in bed, up on his knees.

"Dad, can you juggle my fountain pen—and this chair?"

"Easy!"

I tossed them both in at once. The leg of the chair caught the tube running up his nose, but in one motion he caught the chair, jerked out the tube, plus the one from his mouth, and sent them all spinning upward.

"IV stand!" he shouted, scrambling down from the bed. "Gimme room, boy!"

My father was magnificent. He juggled the IV stand in such a way that the tube remained attached to the back of his hand.

"I can juggle my robe and the Gideon Bible too!" he roared.

"I know you can, Dad!"

He juggled those with ease, then snatched up the slippers that had sat forlorn and useless by his bed from the moment he was wheeled in. He juggled the spare blanket that had been neatly folded on the bed next to his, an empty bedpan, my jacket. He danced out into the hall—"Make way!" I hollered—and snatched a nurse's hat and sent it up into the maelstrom. The nurse huffed in anger for a moment, then softened, broke into a grin, and laughed, delighted, "Why, Mr. Vannatta!"

He juggled two empty Coke cans, a stethoscope, a sack lunch, a wheelchair, a son's grief, a mattress pad, a jambox, a Norelco coffee maker. Oh, he was rolling! There was no stopping my dad now! He juggled out the door, into the night, where he juggled a security guard's revolver, a no parking sign, a lilac bush, a drifting cloud, a son's love, the moon and stars and heavens and years and memories never fumbled, never lost. And then he reached down and took me under the arms and threw me up there too, among all those worlds and time, where I rose and fell, rose and fell, always caught by those huge, gentle hands, me, Daddy's bouncing boy.

THETIS, MARY, AND MOTHER

1. Thetis

The ancient Greeks were greatly concerned with armor. After mighty Achilles was done in by Paris, the poets tell us in great detail how Aias and wily Odysseus saved his body from the Trojans. But it was his armor they both were interested in, and Aias slew a herd of sheep in his rage at being denied the prize, then, in shame, slew himself.

Thetis, no doubt, was more interested in the body of her son, but the poets tell us nothing of this. They do not tell us how she wept in relief that he was gone, relief that at last she was freed from the world of men.

She had been unlucky in her men, unlucky in love. Lover, husband, son—she had wanted none of them, suffered them all.

"Thetis! Oh, Thetis!" Zeus had moaned, dry-humping her in the dark shadows of a portico one spring evening on Olympus, his big ham-hands digging into her tender girl's buttocks. "Meet me on Samos—cave—southeast corner—tomorrow—noonish—ahh!"

Hera found out about it, sent old prissy busy-body Prometheus with the tale that Thetis would bear a child greater than his father—one of the most hackneyed ruses on the books but guaranteed to have some effect on Zeus, who was touchy on the subject of patricide. So he agreed to marry Thetis off to Peleus.

Peleus! He spent most of their wedding day vomiting up the fine wine that he drank too much of, undiluted. He had to stand on Hermes' helmet to kiss her—even though she was small for a goddess—and his breath smelled of garlic—garlic!, which to Thetis was decaying vegetable matter, natural corruption, humanity, mortality, death.

She slept with him only once—that was the deal with Hera. After that once Zeus wouldn't want her anymore, Hera knew, nor would any god.

Peleus came to her on their wedding night, his little thing dangling like a pale fig that had grown in the shade. She sighed and lay back, opened her legs. Except for the smell of garlic and stale wine, she would hardly have known he was there. A night breeze wafted through the window. She closed her eyes and imagined great Zeus coming to her as a bull, a swan, a shower of gold. Before Peleus had finished, she was asleep.

She awoke at false dawn—Peleus snoring beside her, his cheek and neck wet with spittle—and wept, not because she was married to a dying man, a mortal, a pitiful thing who could not even throw a good woman in a wrestling match, but because she realized that the true curse of her marriage was yet to come: a son, whom she would not want but would love and pity and grieve for even before his death.

Half-god they would say of Achilles, the mortals, in awe and envy, even though one could no more be a man-god than one could be a virgin mother. To be a mother, you had to suffer the man on you, in you, suffer *garlic,* and to be a man, you must suffer death.

She wanted her son to live forever, dipped him in the river Styx, botched the job, thereafter lived in fear.

He was the butt of jokes. At the age of four he whipped the bully on the block, then ground his heel on a cocklebur and ran to his mama screaming as the boys howled in delight. She took him onto her lap, stroked his head, just as she did years later when Agamemnon took his Briseis. He was a grown man then, but slow-witted, easily confused by Agamemnon's arrogance, old Nestor's pleas for moderation, Athena's sudden appearance in his tent. He ran to his mama.

For a great, hulking brute, he wept easily. History tells us of three times when mighty Achilles wept. He wept at the loss of Briseis, who might, in a different fate, have become his wife, Thetis' daughter-in-law. He wept once more, crawled up into his mother's lap and wept, when his buddy Patroclos was killed by boasting Hector, and he wept when old King Priam knelt before him and conjured up a vision of fathers and sons.

Peleus! That's who Achilles wept for. His *father.* Old garlic-reeking

Peleus who mounted the goddess Thetis one dark night and rut-
ted with his pitiful little dying thing, moving her no more than
a puff of air, as the gods of Olympus snickered into their goblets
of gold. Achilles finally became a man, we say, we are to admire
him most, we say, when he remembered his *father.*

Thetis could have torn her hair.

But that was not her curse. Her curse was to suffer a man on
her, then to watch her little boy die on the dusty plains of Troy,
to see him weep the fourth time, which history does not record:
when the arrow pierced his heel. He wept for the old reason—he
did not want to die any more than Hector had, who ran around
the walls of Troy three times to escape his fate, or Patroclos, wearing Achilles old armor, or Agamemnon, home from the war, with
a robe thrown over him as his wife stabbed him once, twice, thrice.

Neither Homer in the *Iliad,* nor Virgil in his *Aeneid,* nor any of
the minor poets tell us what Achilles felt when he was dying. They
had turned their attentions to something more interesting: armor.
Homer devotes one hundred and forty-five lines to the great shield
alone.

Of Thetis, after the death of her son, the ancients tell us nothing at all.

2. Mary

Once, at a wedding in Cana, when there was no wine, I went to him, my son, and I said, "We have no wine," and he said to me, his mother, "Woman, what have I to do with thee?" His *mother* he said this to. I could have wept.

What have I to do with *thee?*, I should have said. I should have told him about the wind that came in the night and pushed me, blind in the darkness, onto my back, pushed my legs apart, my robes up around my ears, almost suffocating me—a groping, rude, nasty wind. That wind would not take no for an answer.

The word become the wind become the Word, one of them, one of *his* friends said later—Luke I think it was, the brainy one, or maybe my nephew John when one of his fits was on him, his eyes rolling back into his head. I never could understand what they were getting at, all nonsense to me the way they'd talk, Jesus the worst of the lot. He was always a mystery to me.

"Woman, what have I to do with thee?"

The idea of it! If he could have felt that wind, I tell you, he would have known something then! Pushing an innocent girl's legs open that way. I'll never get over it.

If it'd been Gabriel, now, an angel of a man... He was making the rounds then, first to Elisabeth, then me. "Blessed art thou among women," he said, one of the oldest lines. And God help me it might have worked—his hair shone so in the brightening air!—if it'd been him who came in the night. But no. It was a *wind*, I tell you, a cold lover.

I had been popular, all the boys liked me, I could have made a good match, but after the wind came, what could I do? Joseph.

Only a fool would take me in my condition, and that meant Joseph. Stuttering, stammering, clumsy Joseph, who all the children teased, stole his eggs, dropped goat turds in his milk, set fire to the thatch roof of his woodshed. After the shining man Gabriel, how could I let that great klutz put his calloused mitts on me? "I'll marry you, Joseph, but you must promise never to touch me. I'm the child-bride of the Lord."

I grew to pity him, but never to love. It was Jesus I loved from the first. What a bright, gentle lad! He was never a bit of trouble, always minded his mama, would bring me a wild rose when they were blooming by the river, or a bit of honeycomb. How I'd weep when he ran to me with his nose all bloodied by the village bullies. He would never hit back, he was too gentle for that.

We doted on one another. That's why I couldn't believe it when he said that thing to me: "Woman, what have I to do with thee?"

It was the rabbis, I guess. They filled him with ideas too big for his sweet little head. I remember once when he was seven, eight, the rabbi caught him in the temple pretending to read the Torah—as if a poor carpenter's son could read!—and kicked him in the backside so hard that he had to sleep on his stomach. I was furious. "Joseph, go give that rabbi a punch he won't soon forget!" I said, but the big cow only mumbled into his beard and did nothing. "It's all right, Mama," Jesus said, always willing to forgive.

But I don't think he ever quite forgave. When he threw that fit in the temple many years later, I think with every kick he gave those oxen and sheep, with every money-changer's table he sent flying, he was remembering the boot of that rabbi.

By then I had lost him. He'd started into that son-of-God business—I'll take my share of the blame for that—and I knew it was only a matter of time until they would have enough on him.

He was never strong, and he lasted only three hours on the cross. I thank the Lord for that. Still, what a thing for a mother to witness...

Mothers should not outlive their sons. I didn't want to, I prayed to God to let me die before my son, I swear I did, but prayers are not meant to be answered. If my prayers had been answered, it would have been Gabriel who came to me that night, and not *wind*.

So Jesus was gone and I was left with Joseph. Sometimes I'd think I'd go insane how he'd go for days on end without saying so much as a word. But it wasn't easy for him either, I know. He never touched me. Only once, when he was old, he came to me, the need scarring his face like an awl, and begged me to lie with him. "Stand there," I said, positioning him at arm's length. "Now, if you can blow me onto my back, blow my robes up, and force my legs apart with your breath alone, I'll let you do what you want." How that man blew! I laughed until the tears ran down my cheeks.

Thinking back, though, I feel sorry for all of us—Jesus, Joseph, and me. It's a hard life. Thank God it doesn't last forever.

3. Mother

She had never felt such a wind, she said, as the one that almost killed her the night before her eightieth birthday. There had been a tornado watch out all day, and the warning sirens went off as she sat down to dinner. She had her own basement, but she did not want to die alone, so she headed across the street to the Smith's. There wasn't a breath of air when she came out of the house, but before she was halfway across the street, the rain fell like a great river turned on end. Then the wind hit just as she was trying to cross the rain-gorged ditch left by a gas-main repair crew. She couldn't get up out of the ditch and would have died there if Mr. Smith hadn't run out into the storm and pulled her to safety.

How she laughed about it afterward!—but I could tell it had frightened her. Once the bravest of women, she's frightened often now.

Her eightieth birthday has hit her hard. Seventy had not been bad, she had handled seventy, and sixty was a breeze. She worked forty-four hours a week at sixty—she could do forty-four hours a week standing on her head!—had her own teeth at sixty, and Uncle Arthur (arthritis) hadn't begun to pay his visits yet. Fifty? Why, she couldn't even remember fifty, it'd been that easy, a snap. Forty, though, that'd been the hard one. "I thought I was finished at forty," she'd tell us over and over again. What "finished" meant she never said because a mother can't mention certain things to her children, but it is easy enough to figure out.

She'd had enough of us—children—by then anyway. We had all been a surprise, she told my wife once, we were all unexpected. Her last pregnancy came when she was thirty-seven. She thought it was a tumor. I would like to think that she was grateful to find that it was me, and not death, growing in her. But one can't be sure. She has always been an independent woman, and perhaps she thought of each of us as a violation and an encumbrance.

By her fortieth birthday I would have been walking, talking, and potty trained, and she would be finished with conceiving. "Get a job. Work just long enough to pay off the new car," my father pleaded. So she went to work and abandoned me, howling and clinging to her skirt, with Mrs. Pierce.

The new car was a loathsome gray 1950 Pontiac. The earliest nightmare that I can recall was of my mother in that Pontiac driving up to Mrs. Pierce's house to fetch me. Slowly, slowly, it rolled down the drive, then magically overturned. My mother stared up at me, eyes open, dead.

The dream is easy enough to interpret: parental abandonment, etc., etc. But I don't think I was as resentful as the dream would seem to indicate. I was afraid of *everything* as a child, and the nightmare was just one more howling demon among the thousand that haunted me.

I was more resentful years later, perhaps, when she left me with Mrs. Burton—months and months—as I recovered from rheumatic fever. Mrs. Burton popped her gum and watched soap operas hours on end as I lay on the bed, paralyzed with hatred and boredom. I began to read. Classic Comics were my favorites, and my first Classic was the *Iliad*. Since I had not read the original, I would hardly have missed Thetis, who is not mentioned in the Classic *Iliad*. But I was moved by great Achilles' tears as he thought of his father, old Peleus.

My father was big as God. With one of his great fingers he'd lift me into the air as I shrieked in delight. We were inseparable; as we walked side by side, I'd run four steps to match his one long slow stride. I'd find dark, dry places for him to hide his cigarettes— from *her*. Mother was our common enemy. She seemed to be always in a rage against him. It took me years to realize that it was rage born of fear. We were both afraid for him.

My father was dying all my life. His first heart attack came when I was three. My mother would have been forty then. "I thought I was finished at forty," she'd say. My sister and I would think of Jack Benny and laugh, but it was no joke to her. *What* was finished? Some things can't be contemplated by a son: My father, big as a bull, snorting in lust or stalled in impotence over... No no. Some things cannot be contemplated by a son.

She was always in a rage at his foolhardy ways: he would not cut back at work, would not lose weight, insisted on hauling the old chifferobe out to the back yard and trying to break it up himself instead of letting me do it, as Mother ordered. "What kind of man they must think I am," he wheezed, rubbing his left arm and eyeing the neighbors' kitchen windows as he surrendered the ax to me.

He chewed garlic—read in an article it was good for the health, he said, but it was really to hide the odor of cigarettes on his breath. At some point—when I was eleven, perhaps, or twelve—I stopped helping him hide his Chesterfields and began helping her find them. It was not betrayal. I was growing more and more afraid for him, and I began to understand, if not share, my mother's rage at his heedlessness.

He was afraid, too. He would lie in bed at night taking his pulse, she said, taking it over and over until she would want to scream. It maddened her that a man could fear so much for his life while he ignored his immortal soul—by then he had stopped going to church.

My faith at that time was suspect, too, although I still went to church out of habit. I liked the hymns at least, especially at Christmastime. A nativity scene would be set before the altar. Fat, lugubrious tears would begin to well when I gazed at baby Jesus in the manger. What a fate he was born for, I would cluck sadly. I didn't think of Mary. If I prayed in those days, I would pray for my father to live forever. I did not pray for my mother.

He did not live forever. It was the third heart attack—a bright, cold Sunday morning—that killed him. The night before, trying to make conversation with an indifferent son, he had picked up one of my textbooks and said, "This looks interesting." I shrugged, "It's just a book on mythology."

More and more I took refuge in books; I especially loved the ancient poets. They have a way of coming at the hard things indirectly, spinning good yarns out of what must have been private pain: Homer longing to see his father's face; Aristophanes' son dead at Syracuse; Aeschylus and his jealous wife. But, I wonder now, what do we learn from them, really? Through suffering, wisdom? The suffering I understand, but where in my forty years is the wisdom?

Yes, forty has hit me hard, too. Sometimes I think I'm finished at forty.

She was not quite sixty when my father died. She'd had a lifetime to prepare for it, and she took it well. She worked forty-four hours a week, plus overtime. Sixty had been a breeze for her, and at seventy she still mowed her own yard and shoveled the snow out of her driveway. But now she's eighty, failing, and afraid.

What have I learned to help her die?

I would remind her of her brave deeds. Remember how as a girl fleet-footed as Atalanta you would run down the horses in the winter woods and ride them, laughing, bareback. Do you remember how you beat the flames on your sister's burning dress—with your bare hands, still scarred—and then ran into the woods when the doctor came to change Bernice's dressings? You ran and ran, hoping to outrun her screams, but they always found you, and you would run back and touch her, gently, someplace where she had not been burned. Do you remember when you and Daddy walked across a barely frozen river one Sunday? Just to get to the other side, for no other reason, you were just young and in love and foolhardy and wanted to get to the other side!

* * *

I live in another state now and visit my mother three times a year, at Thanksgiving, News Years, and once in the summer. When we leave after each visit, she will stand in the driveway and wave as we drive down the block to the corner, turn and drive on until we disappear beyond the Wallace's house. She will stand there waving goodbye in the wind, rain, snow. I've given up telling her to go back inside. She's superstitious, obviously, and thinks that waving us on our way will ensure a safe journey. Obviously, she still worries about me. I'm past forty now, have high blood pressure, smoke, don't watch my diet. Probably she's afraid that she'll outlive me.

It just occurs to me that that is what she's been afraid of all along.

CHICKEN IN THE BARN

"Here's one for you," I say to Billy, pushing off with both feet, holding my legs out straight, and letting the swing glide back and forth in the sweet night air. "Think about this one for the Top Ten. Now don't squawk till you've thought about it. How's this. Mitch Ryder and the Detroit Wheels, 'Good Golly Miss Molly.' "

Billy slouches farther down in the aluminum lawn chair, pretends to think hard about Mitch Ryder, but he keeps shooting glances over toward the machine shed where my boy Will is banging away on that godforsaken tractor. Billy and Janet never had any kids.

"She sure like to ba-a-all!" I let out, bouncing up out of the swing and doing a ferocious buck dance for about five seconds, then sitting back down and hammering out the rest of the first verse with the empty beer can on the arm of the swing.

But Billy doesn't join in, just mumbles, "That's a good one, Chuck, cannot be denied. But it ain't no Top Ten."

I dig my heels in and stop the swing, lean forward, prepared to argue. When the rusty chains on the swing stop squeaking, the crickets start back up.

"You ought to think about it, Billy. 'Good Molly Miss Molly' is a hell of a song. Mitch Ryder can really pound them out. If you want my opinion, you're getting a little tight-assed about the Top Ten."

"Look, it's a nice little song, sure, OK, I'll grant you that, but it's derivative, pal. De-ri-va-tive, and you know it. Besides," he says, pointing the beer can at me accusingly, "Mitch Ryder dates from '65, '66. You know the rules."

"Don't point that can at me, you fool! You know an empty beer can's the most dangerous kind!. . . Linda! Bring us out a couple of beers next time you get a chance, OK, sweet thang?"

"Who's gonna be your nigger this time next year?" she hollers back from inside the house.

I laugh and settle back, thinking about the Top Ten Greatest Rock 'n Roll Songs of All Time, a list Billy and I started working on in honky-tonks after we got out of the army in '67.

Billy and I go back a long ways. We grew up on farms not two miles apart, went to grade school and Prospect High together. I began farming right away after graduating in '63 while Billy tried his luck on the party circuit at the university in Fayetteville.

He made it about a year-and-a-half before they got wise to him and bounced his behind back home. I got drafted in 1965, and Billy went ahead and volunteered. We took the same bus to the induction station in Memphis, where I got sent to Ft. Lost-in-the-woods, Missouri, for Basic, and Billy went to Ft. Ord, California. I spent my hitch growing frostbite on my buns outside of Kaiserslautern, Germany, and Bill worked in a supply depot at Cam Rahn Bay and came back with the nicest stereo outfit you ever saw.

The rules of the Top Ten are pretty simple. Rule number one: nobody from the Beatles on can play real rock 'n roll, so no song from the fall of '63 on can be considered for the Top Ten—so that lets out Mitch Ryder, which I know as well as Billy. Rule number two: Billy and me both have to agree on the song and its exact ranking before it's allowed in the Top Ten. There's always gonna be one or two in there by Buddy Holly, a couple by Chuck Berry and Little Richard. Something off the wall may sneak in there depending on our mood. What we mostly argue over is Elvis Presley and the great one, Jerry Lee—the Killer, honey, and don't you forget it. Billy's a pretty good boy most of the time—hell, we named our son after him—but he shows evidence of being tit-fed until he was a teenager by arguing for the Pelvis. No grown man who wore diapers can sing real rock 'n roll is my opinion. (But he loved his mama.)

I'd already tried insulting Elvis, and that didn't work, and violating the rules by nominating Mitch Ryder didn't get much of a rise out of Billy either, not tonight. He's down in the dumps about his dog, Half-pint. Tried to commit suicide, Billy says, by bailing out of the back of the pickup doing a flat seventy mile an hour. Billy'd taken him over to the vets in Marseilles this afternoon.

"Half-pint'll be OK, I bet," I say. Billy gets real attached to his dogs.

"Probably."

"What do you think made him do it, you figure?"

"Saw the handwriting on the wall. Probably read the papers yesterday and saw all about there being so much corn in Illinois and Nebraska that they're piling it up on the edge of the highways, renting airplane hangars to store it in."

I nod. Ain't that always the way of it? Get good weather, good crops, prices go down to where you can't afford to haul it into the elevator. Only time prices are up is when you ain't got any crops. Way it always goes.

"I put everything into corn and soybeans, and Kansas has the biggest year in this decade," Billy grunts. "If I was sitting on all those hogs like you, I'd wake up every morning singing the goddamn 'Star Spangled Banner.' "

"Hogs! Yeh, I'm making a killing. I'm going to buy me a house next door to Jerk Dick Rockefeller."

"Hogs are high."

"They're OK."

"Hogs are *high*."

"They're OK, they're OK. I'll make a little money on 'em. And I'll have a little left over to pay the interest on my loans for this year. And where does that leave me? With enough red ink to paint my house and yours."

"I'd trade places with you."

"Sure you would—this year."

Then we both drop it, the way you'd stop scratching a mosquito bite—not because it stopped itching but because picking at it's only going to draw blood.

Billy raises the can almost to his lips and then sets it back down again.

"Hey, I damn near forgot," he says. "Haul your tired old butt out to my pickup and see what the new day's brung you."

I catch up to Billy as he opens the door of his pickup and starts digging something out from under the seat. "Look what I got you in Conway," he says, handing me a small paper sack. I can tell by the size and shape what's in it. "I was getting that corn-picker worked on, and I stopped off in Mountjoy's Records and Tapes to kill some time. There was that little jewel."

I finger the sack, put off looking inside just for the delicious suspense of it.

"How come you took your corn-picker all the way into Conway? Why not just go into Ferguson's in Marseilles?"

"Ferguson's! I wouldn't let those shit-for-brains work on a nickel yoyo."

There's some bad blood between Ferguson's and Billy over a valve job on a pickup.

I peek inside the sack.

"Lordy lordy. Lord love ya, sweetheart."

Jerry Lee Lewis. "Whole Lotta Shakin' Goin' On."

Billy leans back against the pickup, arms folded across his chest, a broad smile on his face.

"Old Mountjoy says he bought a jukebox at some honky-tonk bankruptcy auction and this big box of 45s come with it. He said a lot of them were so old and scratched up he just give them a toss, but there was this Jerry Lee Lewis there, damn near mint. He can't explain it. I played it. It's real clean. Not a scratch."

"JLL is hell when he's well."

"But he ain't never as well as Elvis."

I hold the 45 up, inspecting it in the glare of the yard light, blow a speck of lint off.

"You're a good man, William Fairchild."

"Ain't I been telling you that all these years?"

"Come on inside and we'll play this eight or nine times."

"Aw, I guess Janet and me'd better be getting on home. Putting up hay tomorrow. . . . Say! I didn't tell you the one about me and her in to McDonald's today in Conway, did I?"

He sits his beer can on the hood of the pickup and leans over on his elbow against the fender.

"This Bronco or whatever you call it—you know, one of them yuppy pickups—pulls in with Massachusetts plates on it, and this couple comes in and sits down at the booth right next to our table. The man starts rubber-necking around, seeing himself some real live Arkansawyers, you know, and starts up a conversation with me. Not long before he finds out I'm a farmer. Well now! If he ain't hit the blessed jackpot. Not only found himself a hillbilly but a *farmer* hillbilly. So to get close, you know, to show he's just a poor slob like me, guess what Boston Charley starts talking about?"

"How down deep he hates niggers just like all us good ol' boys from the South."

"No—that'd probably've been next, I grant you—but no, not yet. He—"

"—wait a minute, one more guess. How he just loves Loretta Lynn."

"Willy Nelson!"

I shake my head.

"Some things never change," I say.

"I don't think there's a single thing that shows the general lack of understanding of the farm problem better than city folks thinking all we do is sit around listening to Country and Western."

"I'd just as soon die."

"Rock 'n roll is where the country meets the city. You'd think folks'd understand that. Hell, Elvis, Buddy Holly, even that degenerate Jerry Lee—"

"—Elvis Presley is the whore that bore you—"

"—were all basically country boys gone to the city. Same for the black singers. Why Bo Diddley, Little Richard—"

He goes on. I've heard it all before, Billy's theory about the connection between rock 'n roll and the farm problem. Hell, I'd probably made up some of it myself. But more and more I can't connect anything to the farm problem. Billy and I, our farms, little farmers everywhere seem to be just green leaves blown off from the branch by a hot hard wind, blowing and tumbling this way and that, not knowing what to do except turn brittle and brown and crumble and die. Got to be a better way. Give it up. Move to Little Rock. Get some work that pays by the hour.

" 'Get a Job,' " I say. "The Silhouettes."

Billy breaks off his tirade, thinks a minutes, nods, "Good song," and starts up again.

Two beers suddenly dangle in front of my face. It's Will. I take the beers and hand one to Billy. Will heads on back to the machine shed, a radio-cassette player dangling from his left hand. In a minute I hear music, or what Will calls music, then the louder ringing of metal against metal.

"Billy!"

It's Janet. I turn just enough to see her in the doorway, silhouetted against the kitchen light. Billy stops, pauses without answering, drums his fingers against the back of the swing. I think I detect the rhythm of "Yakety Yak," the Coasters.

Janet is worried. I can tell it in her voice, see it in the way she's aged too quickly the last few years. Not just the greying hair, but the lines running down her face from the corners of her eyes as if gravity was pulling the slack skin out of shape. She's worried about Billy. He used to be as good a farmer as I knew, but lately he's been slipping. Oh, he still gets things done eventually, but he puts them off, invents excuses for not doing the work when it's ripe to do. Courting disaster.

" 'Funny How Time Slips Away,' " I say.

"Willy Nelson!" Billy laughs, then grows serious, thinks about it.

"A good song," he says—so softly that I can hardly hear him against the bad music coming from the shed, Will pounding away at the tractor, and the crickets—'a real good song, but it ain't rock 'n roll."

*   *   *

Billy and Janet have left for home. Will's tape has run out in the cassette player, and he hasn't bothered to flip it to the other side. The only sound is the crickets and the softer sounds of Will moving steadily and confidently between the tractor and workbench strewn with tools; the workbench and the canvas spread on the ground and covered with tractor parts, cleaned and oiled; the canvas and the tractor.

It's an International Harvester. We bought it only two years old back in the '70s when prices were really good, when farmers started buying up acres they didn't have time to work, buying machinery at high interest rates because they thought two years of good prices would last forever, let them live a little like other people, take a vacation once every five years, air condition their homes. International Harvester, a big son-of-a-bitch, big enough to go to war on. Then one day in 1981 it started spewing oil all over creation, threw a rod and somehow managed to crack the block—just sat down and died. It was going to cost over a thousand dollars, maybe over two thousand—and who knows what now?—to get it fixed. Bad times had already hit then, it cost more to put a crop in the ground than you could get once you sold it, so I just let the IH sit. There it sits today.

But Will took an automotive course in at Prospect High—didn't have any such thing when Billy and I were there—and a few months ago he decides to try to fix it up himself. Every few days you'll see him lugging in some part that he finds God knows where—buys himself—and you're liable to find him in the machine shed any hour of the day or night hammering away on the damn thing. I keep telling him he doesn't have a Chinaman's chance of getting that lemon running, but he won't listen. He was born not listening to me, I think.

I watch him for a few minutes. He doesn't know I'm there, standing just beyond the perimeter of light. Then I say, loudly, like I've just walked up on him,

"Will! You better leave that for tonight. You've got to be over to Billy's early in the morning to help him put up hay."

He looks around in my direction, but his glance doesn't quite reach me.

"I'll just be a little while longer. I'm not tired yet anyway."

"Come on inside. This is a waste of time, I've told you and told you. Besides, I've got something to show you."

"What?" he says, sounding a little suspicious.

He's half-a-head taller than me—gets his size from the Graham side of the family. If you saw us from a distance, you'd probably think I'm the boy and he's the daddy.

"Got something for you to hear."

"Oh," he grunts, his shoulders slumping, "a new record."

"Yep, an all-time great, currently pushin' hard for number one."

"Jerry Lee Lewis," he says. "I've heard them all."

" 'Whole Lotta Shakin'!"

"I've heard it before."

Wrong generation. I know it's only natural, but I feel myself getting angry. The way he moves so surely among the pieces of that disaster that grinds my guts every time I think about it. Listens to that trash he calls rock and doesn't understand a blessed thing about what the world is about to do to him.

"Come on in and listen to it, Jesus H. Christopher!... It's an original. Mint."

He sighs and lays down the Crescent wrench.

"OK, I'll be in as soon as I get this stuff straightened up."

"Leave it. Do it tomorrow."

He moves slowly about the shed, putting everything back in place.

* * *

I've got the record on, and the song's halfway over by the time Will gets back into the house.

He waits patiently for the song to end, then, politely, listens while I play it again from the beginning.

When it's over, he nods.

"Yeh, I've heard that one before."

* * *

First thing the next morning, I notice doing my chores that the water line to the hog lots has gotten stopped up, so I spend half the morning hauling water down to thirsty piggies, then the other half taking the line apart trying to find out where the Sam Hill it's blocked.

It's after one o'clock before I'm finished, and I get back to the house just before Harold Crow drives up with the mail. He hands a few bills and circulars out the window to me, then a catalogue.

"Looks like another college catalogue," he says. "That one's from Purdue University. I thought Will'd already decided to study farming up at the U of A."

"That's what you thought, was it?. . . Well, don't take any wooden postcards."

I walk off toward the house.

Son-of-a-bitch got handed a hundred dollar bill every time he minded his own business he'd starve to death in a week.

When I get inside, Linda is washing up the dinner dishes.

"Didn't even wait dinner on me? Now I'm real happy."

"Will got back from Billy's around noon, so we ate then. There's roasting ears on the stove and a tuna sandwich in the fridge. Jar of pickled beets in there too."

"How come he's back from Billy's already? They can't be half through putting up hay yet."

"Will said something about Billy getting a wild hair about something or other and taking off for town."

I think of Janet, the worry in her voice. Billy's hay was ready

CHICKEN IN THE BARN

to put up a week ago. Weather's perfect, hot and dry. But Billy piddles and piddles. Janet, how she's aged fast.

*   *   *

I find Will sitting on the fender of the pickup, looking down the slope at our bottom land. This time of year the creek's down, and the bottom land stretches out flat and fertile, so rich you'd think if you threw a nickel down on it dollar bills would spring up in neat green rows.

I know what he's thinking.

I tell him about the water line, then ask him about Billy.

"Took off into town to take out a loan."

"What kind of loan?"

"Wants $5,000 to build him one of those galvanized hay barns."

"What for? He's got enough room in his old barn."

Will shakes his head.

"Huh uh, nope, not for next year anyway. He's going back to nothing but square bales next year. Says he loses too much to spoilage on the big round ones."

I don't know whether to laugh or cry. Billy was one of the first around here to go to the round bales. For years, like most of us he'd hire someone to come in once a summer and bale it up for him, leave it lay in the field. Then half a dozen years ago he bought a baler himself, cost enough to feed half the population of India. He couldn't possibly have that thing paid off by now. And $5,000 for a new barn?

"Five thousand dollars won't half buy a barn like he's thinking about," is all I can think to say.

"No sir."

Then I remember what I came out here for. I pull the catalogue out of my pocket, hand it toward Will.

"Look what come in the mail today. This one's from Purdue University. One of the best engineering schools in the country."

Will slides off the fender, takes a step or two in the direction of the creek.

"I didn't order that."

"I know you didn't order that, but you can goddamn look at it, can't you?"

He reaches back toward me and takes it, lets it dangle at his side.

"Dad, you know as well as I do that I'm going to Fayetteville. I'm already accepted and enrolled. I start school in six weeks—you know that."

"Sure you're going to Fayetteville—for now—but in a couple of years after you get all that English and fingerpainting and such stuff out of the way, then you're going to want to get into your real studies and—"

"—I'm going to study agriculture."

"—you should study your options, that's all I'm saying. Engineering—your science grades were real good—business. Get into that computer stuff maybe. Purdue, now—"

"I'm going to study agriculture at the University of Arkansas at Fayettevile."

"Yeh, and you're not going to have a pot to piss in or a window to throw it out of! You'll die beat, broke, and stupid, just like your old man."

"You're not doing so bad. We're not doing so bad."

I do a little dance in the dust, looking for something to kick hard. I'd kick the pickup, but it's not all the way paid for.

Before I can really let loose, Will walks around to the door of the pickup, reaches in, and pushes the button on his radio-cassette player. I stand there a minute and listen to the music and try to calm down.

"What do they call that?" I say.

"Tears for Fears."

"Tears for Fears? Sweet Jesus I'm comin' home. Is that what passes for rock 'n roll these days? Take me now, Lord, take me now."

"Dad, you're living in the past."

"Living in the past? No man thinks about what's coming down the road more than I do."

"Yeh, but you're always jumping out of the way. When it comes down the road, I want to be riding on it."

He snaps the music off and starts jogging down the hill toward the bottom land. In a minute, he's almost lost from sight behind the brush that floated up the last time the creek got out, after all the rain in early June.

I know what he's thinking, but Otto Jobst tried it, and look what happened to him. Jobst had fifty, sixty acres of bottom land not half a mile up the creek. He'd plant it in corn, soy beans, whatever, then when the crops were looking like a million dollars the creek would get out and take everything. So Jobst decides to build an earthen dike all along the creek there, hires a guy to come in on a bulldozer and do it for him. The guy's out there every day for a month and a half, and, yes, the dike keeps the water back. But that year—it was 1980—it goes sixty-seven straight days through the summer without getting more than a half inch of rain in any one day, and Jobst loses his crops, can't pay off the loan he took out to pay through the nose for the bulldozer, then loses his farm.

Will thinks he can clean off the brush and build his dike by getting the International Harvester running. He thinks the IH is big enough to push dirt if he can jerryrig some kind of plow that he bought cheap at an auction onto the front. It lies under a tarp up against the machine shed. Once a week or so Will takes a stiff wire brush to the rust that keeps growing on it. By the time he gets the IH running, he'll have that plow scraped clean away.

I think he's in for pain. I think he's going to wind up investing more than he can stand to lose. You shouldn't have to sell your soul. In times like these you shouldn't have to sell your soul.

* * *

It's close to 4:30 in the morning before I find Billy. He's outside a private club called the White Horse, sitting on what looks like a felled telephone pole that borders the east edge of the parking lot and keeps the drunks from driving off into the ditch. He has a big grin on his face as I sit down next to him on the pole, but I can tell he's been crying.

"Finally found a juke box that has some Elvis on it," he says, nodding over toward the White Horse. "Played 'Heartbreak Hotel' seventeen straight times, then they kicked me out."

"I'd've throwed you out after about two."

Janet had called me out of bed after midnight. She was worried sick about Billy. He'd gone off in an awful state, and she was afraid he'd get himself in a car wreck. I'd checked everyplace I could think of around Prospect and then Marseilles, but I didn't spot him until on a whim I slipped across into Broyles County.

"I done something real stupid today," he moans, hanging his head down between his knees.

"You mean I get to go on a bender everytime I do something stupid? Hot damn, I got some good times ahead of me!"

"Know what I did today?"

"Yeh, I heard."

"Went out and borrowed $5,000 and then threw it away with both hands."

"You're not the first—"

"Janet deserves better than me."

"I wouldn't—"

"She always wanted a little girl."

Suddenly, I see Billy at the Sophomore sock hop, 1961. It's May, it's hot, and him and me are standing underneath the basketball goal with our armpits full of sweat, trying to get up the guts to ask somebody to dance. Then he just takes off, straight across the gym floor and right up to Janet Schleissman. In a minute, they're dancing to Buddy Holly, "Peggy Sue." Look how they're going at it! Look at them go!

I stand up.

"I'll be back in a minute."

I head over to the White Horse. When I get to the door, I stop for a minute, wipe at my eyes. Then I go in and order two Buds.

"You ain't a member, are you fella?" the bartender asks me. "This here's a private club. You want to drink, you got to buy a membership card—only set you back five bucks."

"Look," I say, "I got a friend out there dyin' hard, and I just want to drink a beer with him before he's gone, OK? Now be a human being and give me a couple of goddamn Buds."

When I get back outside, Billy is getting heated up on "Heartbreak Hotel." I sit down and hand him a beer.

"I thankee! I'll pay you back just as soon as the crop comes in—good Lord willin' and the creek don't rise."

We take a long drink apiece, and I try out a little "Heartbreak Hotel" myself.

"You're lucky," he mutters, not letting me finish the first verse.

"Yeh, I know. I went with hogs and you went with soy beans and corn. It'll even out—always does."

"I don't mean that. I mean. . .Will."

"Oh. Well. Yeh, he's a good kid, but awful dumb."

"He's smarter than the both of us put together."

"Hell now. You know what he was listening to today? Something called Tears for Fears."

"Well, who knows. Maybe they tell the truth. You know, I been thinking. I think that's what makes good rock 'n roll good. It tells the truth. You ever listen to this Tears for Fears bunch?"

"Not really."

"Maybe you ought to."

Maybe I should. But not now, later. Now I'm getting into "Heartbreak Hotel." Not a bad song. Not bad at all, even for the Pelvis. Billy argues it for number one quite a bit, but I won't have any of that, of course. Not even Top Ten, because it's not rock 'n roll. It's just a ballad. But not bad. And tonight, if he wants it for the Top Ten, he can have it there. For tonight we'll put it right there at number one. Tonight, I'll give him whatever I can.

* * *

It's already getting light out by the time I get back home. I'm dead tired, just beat all the way down. I open the pickup door and hear the *ping ping* of metal against metal coming from the machine shed and I'm mad before I hit the ground.

I head across the lot toward the shed, getting ready to really let Will have it. Wouldn't surprise me if he didn't take advantage of me being gone to work all night on that IH. The waste.

I get halfway across the lot, and then the sound of hammering stops, and then I hear the music. Tears for Fears? I'm not sure. I can't place it. Then in another second the music stops and then I flinch as a terrific explosion rocks the machine shed. I start to run forward, but then I stop.

The explosion doesn't stop, it goes on and on. And then I understand—it's not an explosion at all.

The machine shed is almost black, silhouetted against the rising sun. And then out of the blacker mouth of the shed it comes— the International Harvester, roaring across the lot with Will high atop grinning wildly and waving his free hand like a bronco rider sprung from the chute.

I back up fast as the huge tires of the IH roll by me throwing up so much dirt that I can't even see Will as he shouts down at me through the cloud of dust.

"Chicken in the barn, Dad! We're gonna have chicken in the

barn!" I think is what he's yelling.

"Go, Will, go!" I holler, suddenly so goddamn proud it hurts awful.

He turns out of the lot and then really lets it out as he rides off down the road in the direction of the bottom land.

I stand for a moment, watching him moving away from me. Then I turn and head for the machine shed. I don't know what it is I'm going to hear, but I sit down right there on the ground, cradling the radio-cassette in my arms, push the PLAY button, and begin to listen.

THE WRONG TIME

It was right at half past noon when Jack Echoff came out of his house and walked just a little ways up Main Street before raising the pistol he held dangling at his side and shooting Willy Ochs in the forehead. After it was all over they found the TV still running in Jack's kitchen, tuned to Channel 4, Little Rock, so folks knew what must have happened. Jack'd been watching the noon news and just got fed up, that was plain. Just couldn't take any more. Easy to figure, easy to understand. Could happen to anyone—there but for the grace of God...

It was a bad break for Willy Ochs, though. The bullet from the .25 hit him right in the middle of the forehead, right at the hairline, a glancing blow that made a little furrow through his hair, just creasing his skull. Willy went straight back like his heels were hinged to the sidewalk. The back of his head hit the doorjamb of Miss Lucy's World of Gifts, and it was that, not the bullet, that gave him the concussion, the headaches and dizzy spells for the next couple of weeks.

("Thunk! It hit solid," Miss Lucy said. "Just like that. Thunk! I look up and there he lays." Miss Lucy didn't see the actual shooting, though. George Cole had seen it all from his barber shop, in front of which Jack Echoff had stopped and fired. "Went down like a pole-axed steer. I figured he was long gone from this world," George explained, over and over. Bud Yates was working at the Skelly bulk station across the street at the time, and he had seen it all too. A few others in Prospect claimed to have seen it, but Bud, George, and Miss Lucy were the only ones folks generally believed. Give Miss Lucy credit: She never once claimed more than her fair share of the story. "Thunk! Solid. There he lay, like a dead man." Bud Yates had actually seen the most. From the other side of Main Street he'd seen the pistol dangling from Jack Echoff's right hand. "His arm hung straight down, like it was paralyzed. It looked *grey* to me, like a piece of dead meat. That's what I can't get out of my head—how that arm looked *grey*, like all the blood was gone. Then he raised it." From the first, Bud didn't like to talk about it much. "Whew! I ain't seen nothing like that before, and hope never to again. I couldn't take a whole lot of that." George Cole was different. He'd tell it over and over. He got more mileage out of not seeing the gun than Bud Yates did seeing it. "I didn't see the gun at first, didn't know he had one. Then it came up. I'll tell you what—it sends a shiver through me thinking about it even now. There's Jack, just walking along like you or me. Then he stops right outside my window, not six feet from the end of my nose. Then up comes the gun. Wham! One shot. I turned and looked up Main Street. It starts to curve around there just this side of Miss Lucy's, you know, so I could see Willy plain. He was already down. Went down like a pole-axed steer, the way Miss Lucy tells it. I took one look and said, that boy's gone.')

Later, most people said that Willy Ochs would have been better off if the bullet had killed him.

The county sheriff didn't look around much for motives. Everybody knew the way Jack was, and with the TV on it was obvious what had happened. Jack didn't have anything against Willy—nobody did—Willy was just the first one Jack came up against. "I'd call it just your classic case of being in the wrong place at the wrong time," the sheriff said.

After he fired the shot Jack Echoff walked on past the barber shop and turned into the vacant lot between the barber shop and Miss Lucy's. "He walked right by me," George Cole would say. "I wasn't scared. Not that I'm a brave man, I'm not saying that. George Cole doesn't have a shitting ounce of brave in him. But I wasn't scared. It was easy to see that Jack was finished with it. That shot had done it, and that was all she wrote."

Well, not quite. They heard another shot two minutes, maybe three, later. Jack had walked on through the lot to the dirty, weedy, trash-strewn area between the backs of the Main Street stores and Red Fork creek. He'd sat down with his back against a sweet gum that leaned out over the creek, maybe sat for a minute staring at the water. ("He liked to fish," his neighbor, Albert Sanders would say. "About the only thing he did like. Maybe he give that creek a last look. Who knows?") Then he put the pistol up to his temple and pulled the trigger. They found him with his back against the tree, his head fallen down on his chest. His right eyeball had come out of the socket and hung down on his cheek a bit. Mostly it was the men of the town who knew that. They'd mention it to one another, but they wouldn't talk about it in front of the women and children. It gave a sort of bad taste to the whole thing—the eye did—but other than that folks didn't hold much against Jack. "He did what he was going to do, then paid for it," George Cole said. "No lawyer pleading insanity, then you and me paying for a few years vacation in one of the country clubs that passes for a prison these days. No sir. Did it, then wrapped it up, neat and tidy."

That was Willy Ochs' problem—he couldn't get the whole thing wrapped up. You'd expect a man to have a bad moment or two after a thing like that happened to him, but things kept on getting worse for Willy long past the time when you could rightfully expect folks to sympathize, long past the point of understanding. It wasn't like folks were hard on Willy, just the opposite. They'd give him a lot of sympathy, and mean it. When he'd shake his head in amazement and say, "Why me? I never did a solitary thing to that man. I didn't hardly know who he was," someone would be sure to clap him—not too hard—on the back and say, "It wasn't you, Willy. It didn't have nothing to do with you. Jack Echoff would've shot Jesus Christ if he'd've run into him first that day." And the first couple of weeks, when he was still having his headaches and dizzy spells, someone would be sure to jump up and give him a seat when he came in to the Y'All Come Inn for breakfast. Someone would be sure to ask him how he was doing, too, but they stopped that after awhile because he'd always tell them. He wouldn't just say, "Oh, I'm fine, I'm OK," like you'd expect, but he'd tell you about his latest dizzy spell, his headaches, squinting around the cafe to see if anybody looked like he was in need of a bit more explanation. It got hard to look him in the eye after awhile.

The best explanation for Willy people could think of was the children. Not that they were intentionally mean, but you'd have to admit that they didn't give Willy a lot of rest. "Show us where he shot you in the head, Mr. Ox," they'd say. And for awhile he'd show them. He'd bend down and solemnly pull back the sparse, greying hair of his widow's peak and show them the little furrow—red like a streak of lipstick at first, then almost invisible—that ran from the edge of his hairline about two inches before it disappeared off the top of his head. It didn't take him long to get enough of it, though. (He and his wife had never had any kids, or it probably wouldn't have bothered him as much, that's what folks figured.) When he'd see them coming he'd sort of flinch like a dog that's been kicked once too often, and when they'd say, "Show us where you got shot, Mr. Ox," he'd snap, "*Ochs, Ochs,* not *Ox!* Oh, leave me alone."

(His name had always been a sore point with him. He'd explain it politely to you, almost apologetically but with a note of exasperation in his voice: "It's not *ox.* Not *o-x.* It's *o-c-h-s.* Like this—Ochs. Ochs." And he'd say it over and over, but nobody could ever hear the difference. To humor him you'd say, "Oh, I get it, sure," and twist your mouth around and say "ox" in some strange way, and he'd smile, embarrassed, too polite to show that you hadn't gotten it at all, not at all, and he'd shrug and say, "Well. . ." After the shooting a person or two would recollect the business with his name and nod wisely, "There was the sign. Anybody who'd get that upset over a little thing like that. . ." Others would defend him. "*Upset?* Who ever saw Willy upset? He just wanted you to get the name right, that's all. Can't blame him for that." "*Blame?* Who said anything about blame? All I said was. . ." And it'd go on.)

Margo Morrison, the home ec teacher at the high school, said Willy's problem was the mid-life crisis. "The male version of the change of life, you might say. This all hit him when his self-esteem was already being threatened. Here he is, what, forty-five, fifty, no children, still lives in the same little house, still has the same little job, and what's the future hold? More of the same dreary thing. Being shot just opened the door, you might say, for all those insecurities to well up out of his unconscious."

It's hard to imagine how one person could rub more people the wrong way than Margo Morrison. She'd gotten her teacher's degree only a couple of years ago from Hendrix College. No one held the degree against her. There were quite a few people in Prospect with degrees of one sort or another—all the teachers had them, probably—but most folks had enough sense not to go strutting their stuff when it wasn't called for. "*Edumacation,*" Wes Martin, one of the school bus drivers, would snort. "I've seen all of 'em, and I'll tell you that five minutes in the school of hard knocks is worth a year at Hendrix any day of the week." "Two years. Tell it, Wes." "Edumacation. Shee-it." Hendrix College. You might know that UCA wouldn't be good enough for the Morrisons. They were the ones that put the white picket fence up in front of their farm along Rocktop Road. It would've been different if their house really had been any bigger or nicer than the others out there, but it wasn't, not a bit. A white picket fence in front of the Morrison place was like a bow tie on a hog. Someone had said that.

There was any number of things about Margo Morrison's little speech that didn't sit well with folks, other than the fact of her spouting off in the first place. That male-female business, the change of life and all that, just wasn't necessary and was typical of Margo, who would brag about being a "feminist" at the slightest provocation. ("If she's so damn feminine, how come she ain't got a husband? Answer me that. I'll tell you why. She ain't no feminist, she's a damn *libber,* that's what.") Another thing was that dig about Willy's "little" house. It was out on Rocktop, edge of town, two bedroom, living room, kitchen with a garbage disposal, bathroom with a shower hookup, a room air conditioner. Neat as a pin. What more could you want? That "little" business was inaccurate and just wasn't fair. Willy and his wife kept it up, and after all the wind damage last spring Willy'd put a new roof on it. Did the work himself, which surprised folks because he didn't get many callouses on his hands in his job. And what about that crack about his "little job"? He may not have been rich, but bookkeeping at the feed store was a respectable enough job, even if women had been doing it for as long as people could remember, up until Willy took it over. Besides, how many people around Prospect were rich? Abe Lawrence, the district attorney for Buchanan County, lived in Prospect, but his money came from the government, so folks considered it kind of tainted in a way, sort of borrowed, not quite his own. And Dutch Grimes' farm was worth well over half a million, they said, but they also said he was 700,000 in debt. That kind of rich you can keep, welcome to it. Willy Ochs might not be getting rich, but he paid his bills, he didn't owe a red cent to anybody.

(And what about that name? *Margo!* Who needed a name like that? Let her take that name to Chicago or New York! She'd fit in good there.)

Willy had his own explanation for what was wrong with him, but nobody could make much sense of it. "Here I am one day walking along, just being Willy Ochs, and all that meant, all Willy Ochs was for forty-nine years, and then that business with Jack Echoff happens. Then what am I? I'm not Willy Ochs anymore, not the one I was for forty-nine years. Now I'm one thing—I'm the guy that Jack Echoff shot. That's it. People won't forget it and they won't stop thinking about it. Tell the truth. What's the one thing you think of when you see me? Sure. That's all I am. You start thinking that people are watching you all the time, that the eyes of the world are on you, remembering that one thing. You start feeling nekkid. I feel like I'm nekkid all the time. I'll tell you something—I know what a woman that's been raped feels like. She feels like nothing she's ever been or done means anything anymore, 'cause all she is or will be is a raped woman. I can understand that now. I might as well have been raped."

Even though they didn't much follow what he was talking about, folks would hear Willy out until he got to that last part, then they'd start to fidget. It wasn't comfortable listening to that kind of talk, it just wasn't necessary. "There's never been a woman raped in Prospect in the history of the world," Mildred Cross said, so indignant her eyes fairly snapped when she talked, "never. And he has to go talking like that. I'll tell you, I'm a Christian like everybody else and I feel as sorry for Willy Ochs as the next person, but it's time he started getting back to normal."

But Willy didn't get back to normal. Things actually got worse for him after the headaches and dizzy spells passed. While he was still having them, they gave him something to talk about, and talk he would. Folks had never heard Willy talk so much. The speech where he explained what was wrong with him—what George Cole came to call his "nekkid and raped speech"—was the longest stretch of talking anyone had ever heard from Willy. He'd always been on the quiet side, a shy kind of man—when you thought of Willy Ochs you thought of him standing off to the side a little bit and smiling, friendly, a likeable guy, but not one to volunteer much. But the headaches seemed to open something in him, and he'd talk and talk trying to explain. Then when the headaches stopped and he still wasn't back to normal, that's when he came up with his "nekkid and raped" speech. He only gave that one three or four times, then he clammed up. (Maybe he'd heard about Ray Jacks' crack: "Ol' Willy seems to enjoy speculating on that rape business a little too much to my way of thinking," Ray'd wink, elbowing Chick Grimes, who grinned uncomfortably. Ray Jacks was never worth a damn, never. None of the Jackses were.)

So Willy quit talking. Instead, he began to cry. He didn't do it constantly, he'd go for days at a time sometimes without crying, at least in public. But every once in a while, every few days, someone would see him walk down the street, then stop and look around like he was confused, like he'd forgotten where he was or like he was trying to remember something, then he'd bury his face in his hands and he'd cry in great shaking sobs like something old and rusty had busted loose in a deep hurting place in him. Cry and cry until folks couldn't stand to watch anymore and they'd turn away, back into their home or into the nearest store or even get in their car and ride, leaving Willy in the center of nothing, like everybody in the vicinty had died and Willy grieved to be among the dead.

Even the children, who are quick to pick up on something like that and can be downright cruel at times, let's admit it, even the children, as much as they wanted to ask him all over again about being shot, started to shy away from him. He was easy to shy away from. If he'd see a child coming in his direction—even by accident—he'd turn and head the opposite way. Sometimes he'd make it almost all the way to Main Street, then turn and walk back home in a sort of stiff-legged gait like he was trying to hold himself back from breaking into a run. "He'd make it a little less and less each day," his next-door neighbor, Leona Riley, would tell the women in the Eastern Star. "I would see him walk on past the house from the kitchen window where I'd be putting up vegetables, you know. At first he'd make it on out of sight down towards town. Then later he'd only get to the end of the block and stand there like a little boy whose folks had told him not to cross the street by himself. He'd look kind of cute, really. Then he couldn't get past the middle of the block, just stand there and look down at the end of the block like he was half scared to death. It like to broke my heart. Finally, one day I opened up my window and hollered out, 'Hon, you better come in here and let me pour you

a big glass of buttermilk.' " (Leona Riley could get away with calling a married man 'hon' because of her age and, well, just because
she was Leona. Not everybody could, of course, but nobody'd think
a thing about it with Leona. It didn't do much good with Willy,
though.) "I didn't mean that man a speck of harm—not with the
cross he had to bear. But when I called out he looked at me like
a wild man and fairly ran back to his house. That was the last I
seen of him until the day he went off to do away with himself."

It really didn't catch anybody by surprise. Folks had been expecting something like that. He'd tried to go back to work after the
headaches and the dizziness passed, staying for a couple of hours
some days, even making it until noon once, but it hadn't worked
out. His last day he seemed like he'd almost gotten over the hump.
He fiddled with some papers and pecked away at the adding
machine, then jumped up at about ten that morning to help wait
on customers at the desk like he used to. "Gimme fifty pounds
of pellets for my dogs, Willy. That hole in your head's damn near
healed up, ain't it?" Willy had stared at Little Mick Jackson for
just a second, with a sort of sad look on his face, then he turned
like he'd decided something, shut off the adding machine, walked
out the door, and that was his last day of work at the feed store.
('Now look," Little Mick said, "I like Willy as well as the next guy,
but if you can't even make a little small talk around the guy, why
hell. A body can't go around walking on eggs all your life, you just
can't do it.')

"I felt real bad about having to let Willy go," Karl Meier, the man-
ager of the feed store, said, "If it'd been up to me he could have
taken a month, two, six months, heck, whatever he needed to get
over his little problem. If I could've done it I'd've kept on sending
over his paycheck until he got all that business straightened out—
that's what I would've liked to have done. But you know how the
business has been. Two summers of hot and dry, then nothing but
rain all this spring—heck, I've been carrying half the county on
my books. You wouldn't believe the red some of the farmers around
here have run up. What can you do? You can't get blood from a
turnip. I can't foreclose on somebody's farm like a doggone banker
can. Wouldn't if I could. I'm not that kind."

When Leona Riley saw Willy Ochs walk by her house with the
gun in his hand, the first thing she did was call up her grandson,

Clark Riley, who was the town marshall. "He's got a gun and he's gonna do something bad, most likely to hisself," Leona had said to Clark's wife, Clark being out of the office at the time. Then Leona had run over to the Och's house and opened the front door without knocking and found Mary Ochs crying on the sofa. Later, she'd confided to Leona that what had sent Willy out of the house was her hollering at him. She just couldn't take it any more, him day after day pacing around the house, peeking out from behind the curtains, then more and more lately just sitting at the kitchen table staring at the linoleum like he could read some long sorrowful story there—and Mary wasn't used to having him under foot all day anyway, under the best of circumstances. "Do something, Willy, do something!" she'd screamed, not even planning it, and he'd stood up and knocked over the chair and stared at her wild like she was coming at him with a butcher's knife. Then he ran out of the room, crying like a dropped baby, and Mary'd stumbled into the living room and collapsed onto the sofa, weeping, where Leona found her.

"He didn't have the gun out by the time he got to my place," George Cole said. "He must have stuck it inside his shirt or something. He just walked on by, and I hardly took notice of him, I didn't even have time to nod or wave before he was gone, and I didn't even know anything was up until I saw Clark Riley drive by real slow in his patrol car. What I can't figure though is how Willy came to be walking up from that direction. He lives down the other way, down the far end of Rocktop, but he was walking up from this direction, you know, the same way Jack Echoff had come that day."

After she took Leona's call, Clark's wife, Lu, got Clark on the CB. Clark had driven fast up Rocktop to the Ochs place, then slowly back down toward Main, stopping two or three times to ask people if they'd seen Willy. Clark had just passed the barber shop when George Cole called out after him. ("Well, it hit me all of a sudden, you see. What it was was this. First there's Willy Ochs walking by, kind of stiff and dazed like one of those zombies or something, the way he's been most of the time lately, then the marshall drives by slow, rubber-necking around like he's got his eye out for something. Now this was only a little bitty bit after Willy walks by, but when I turn to see where he's got to, he's nowhere to be seen. He could've ducked in to Miss Lucy's but somehow I didn't think so. You know how you get one of those feelings? Anyhow, that was when I stuck my head out the door and called to the marshall.'')

George was pointing toward the lot and shouting that Willy was heading for the creek. Marshall Riley slammed on the brakes, threw open the door, jumped out, and nearly got run over by Bobby Yates, who was barreling up Main in his pickup. Clark waved Bobby out of the way and ran across the empty lot. He wasn't sure which way to turn. He'd been fishing over on Greer's Ferry Lake the day the Jack Echoff business occurred, and he didn't know the exact spot where Jack had made an end of it. It didn't take Clark long to find him, though, sitting at the base of the sweet gum. He had the barrel of the gun pressed into his temple. His jaw was working like he was chewing on something hard and sticky, and his eyes were clenched tight. He kept pushing the barrel against his temple, hard, then taking it away. His trigger finger was white as a piece of chalk.

"Come on Willy, give me that pistol. You know you don't want to do this."

"Yes I do."

"No you don't, Willy. If you really wanted to, you'd've already pulled the trigger."

". . ."

"Come on, Willy, give me the pistol. Nobody wants this. Besides, you do this, it'll make a lot of trouble for me. You wouldn't believe the paper work."

"Oh."

Willy handed him the gun.

It was almost two weeks before Willy tried it again. ('No," Marshall Riley said, "I didn't confiscate his pistol. I guess a man can put a gun to his head if he takes the notion, long as he don't pull the trigger. I just took the bullets out and gave them and the pistol to Mary and told her to put them somewhere where he wouldn't be likely to pick it up on the spur of the moment. This isn't communist Russia, you know. You can't just confiscate a man's firearms for no good reason.'') Things went pretty much as they did the first time, with a few variations. This time Mary saw him head out of the house with the pistol, and she ran over to Leona Riley's, who called up her grandson at the marshall's office. The problem was that the patrol car was at Bud Yates's getting a front end realignment, and Clark's wife had gone off in the wagon to do an hour's worth of shopping in Marseilles. So Clark had set off up Main Street toward Rocktop at a run. He'd gotten within a block of Willy's house before he figured out that somehow Willy had gotten by him—nobody ever figured that one out—so he had to turn around and run all the way back down Rocktop, then the length, damn near, of Main. By the time he got within a half-block of Miss Lucy's and saw Willy turn into the empty lot, a half-dozen or so men and at least that many kids were jogging along with him, all set on saving Willy from himself.

Willy must have heard them coming because he didn't even pause by Jack Echoff's sweet gum but headed off into the band of woods that grew wider and denser as Main Street curved farther away from Red Fork creek.

Who would have thought that Willy Ochs could move so fast? They heard him crashing through the underbrush ahead of them, but they couldn't quite catch sight of him. "Don't do it, Willy!" they'd shout every once in awhile.

At some point, without anybody meaning it turn out that way, it got funny. You know how it goes—one person starts to laugh, for no good reason at all, then it just sort of catches fire. So in a minute they were all—even Marshall Riley—stumbling through the woods giggling and snorting, hardly able to get out a "Don't do it, Willy!" and finally almost blind with laughter.

It was the laughter—his own—that embarrassed Bill Gilliam enough that he broke off from the rest and veered over closer to the creek instead of just going on straight down the middle of the widening wedge of brush and trees. He and Willy saw each other at the same time. Willy was twenty yards or so ahead, leaning against a hickory tree, panting. When he saw Bill Gilliam, he didn't hesitate but raised the gun to his head. Bill could have sworn that he saw Willy pull the trigger, but nothing happened. Willy stared at the gun for a second like it was a copperhead that'd crawled up into his palm, then turned and ran. They both ran for another twenty or thirty yards. Bill Gilliam stopped first this time—he was past Willy's age, after all, and had been through all that trouble with his kidneys—and then Willy stopped, hand pressed against his side, and raised the gun and, Bill could have sworn it, pulled the trigger. Nothing. They ran, only a few steps this time, until Willy stopped. He was fiddling with the gun as Bill walked up. Willy grinned a grin that could have been cut out of his face with a dull knife, his eyes red and watery like they opened out of a skull full of tears.

"Forgot to load it," he said.

"It wasn't funny, it wasn't a bit funny," Bill Gilliam would say to anybody who mentioned it. His face would get flushed, and he would clench his fists. Bill changed after that. He was never quite the same again, although you couldn't say just how he was different, or how he had been. (Once, though, not long afterward, for the first time since their little boy Donny had been taken from them by the polio thirty years before, Bill, just out of the blue, laid his hand against his wife's cheek, gently.)

Willy never tried to kill himself again after that, although folks would get confused about the number and frequency of attempts and say things like, "Yep, ol' Willy tried to do himself in half a dozen times," or "Ain't Willy Ochs tried to kill himself yet this month?" (But they wouldn't say it around Bill Gilliam, who would have none of it.)

George Cole thought of Willy Ochs' story as one of his better ones, but the fact that it didn't have a proper wind-up bothered him. George liked to think of his barber shop as the center of the town's cultural life and of himself as something like the town chronicler, or historian, or spinner-of-tales—something. The truth was that his barber shop didn't do enough business to be the center of anything. The Clip Joint, a three-seater down on the other end of Main, got most of the men's business. It'd been there longer than George's place for one thing, had built up a more loyal following. George's shop had only the one chair, and George had gotten into the business when barbers with more sense were getting out—in the early '70s, when long hair was finally getting to rural Arkansas. And then there was the sort of tainted air about George Cole left over from the chiropractor business. ('I like George OK, but you and me both know he's slippery—he ain't straight.') He'd opened up a chiropractor office sometime in the early to mid-'60s—hung up a shingle from some school in Florida nobody'd ever heard of—and did a fair business for awhile, but then there started the dirt about Reba Ellway. She started out coming to George's office about once a week, then twice, then folks'd see her heading over there every morning after her husband, Forrest, went to work in the grocery store. The men would wink and say, "Don't know if George's much of a doctor, but he sure must be a hell of a man." But then one day Forrest Ellway locked Reba out of the house with her purse and the clothes on her back, and the last anyone saw of her she was walking south down U.S. 65, head hanging low. After that no woman would go to George, of course, and what few men were inclined to give him the benefit of the doubt shied away after old John Parsons went to George with a stiff neck and afterwards spent the rest of his life with his chin resting on his right shoulder.

So George Cole left off prying on sore necks and took up dishing out bad haircuts and stories about the good people of Prospect, Arkansas. His favorite customers were the rare ones from out of town because then he could roll out all seven of the stories that he kept oiled and polished—three funny ones, three sad ones. He never could figure out which category the Willy Ochs story fit into. ("Now here's a story I don't know whether you'd call it funny or sad," he'd always start out. "You tell me.") He liked the story and told it pretty well, embellishing a little here and there but never outright lying. He'd get uneasy when he got near the end, though, and finally he'd shrug and stammer and admit that, well, the story just kind of petered out. It was like a piece of hemp rope that you were trying to knot, but the ends were all frayed and flying and you just couldn't get ahold of enough to bring it together. You could have done something with the story if Willy had just gone back to his house and shut himself up. Then at least you could say, "And nobody has seen Willy outside his house again to this day." But no. Willy took to roaming the streets again. He'd walk the length of Rocktop Road, then the length of Main Street, sometimes out along U.S. 65, staring around with kind of dead zombie eyes like he didn't know where he was or who he was or anything.

"He walks right by this barber shop two, three, four times a day," George said to the young man from Little Rock, who seemed to be taking more of an interest than most in the story. "You stick around awhile and chances are you'll run into him."

But the man couldn't wait. He'd taken care of his business in

Prospect and on the spur of the moment decided to stop off for a haircut. He needed to get on the road if he intended to make it back to Little Rock by noon. The man paid George his three-fifty, then opened the door and stepped out onto the sidewalk where his car was parked at the curb.

George had just finished putting the money in his billfold—he didn't do enough business to need a cash register—when he noticed the man standing in the screen door again, waving him over. The man had an excited, pleased look on his face.

"What's up?" George asked.

"I just saw him!"

"Who?"

"The guy you just told me about. Willy. The zombie . There he is."

George turned to see a figure retreating up Main Street, just past Miss Lucy's now.

"Him? No no. That's not Willy. That's Robert Callison. He works down at the bank. He's probably ten years older than Willy."

That started George off into a new round of explanation about Willy. But before he could really get started, the man from Little Rock began staring off over George's shoulder, then motioned George to be quiet and gave him a big wink. A couple of seconds later the man moved over to the edge of the sidewalk, gestured for George to make room for a pedestrian to pass.

"Willy, the zombie?" the man whispered, jerking his thumb over his shoulder at the retreating figure.

George was dumbfounded.

"Willy Ochs? Him? No. No! Ha! Why, dang! That's the mayor of Prospect, mister. That's Harlon Young. Hell now!"

George had the notion to take this Little Rock fellow by the collar and march him out Rocktop Road and by God show him Willy Ochs. Maybe that was it. Maybe you couldn't get Willy in a story, maybe you just had to see him.

The man from Little Rock was already climbing into his car, though.

And, really, George didn't have the heart for it anyway. What would have been the use of it, after all? Take him out there, let him see Willy Ochs, maybe even talk to him, and somehow the story would become his, the Little Rock man's, not George's any more. The man would probably go back to Little Rock and tell the story and leave George out of it entirely. George shivered, even though he was standing in the bright morning sun.

He watched the man drive off down the street, then went back into his shop, locked the front door, and flipped the sign around to CLOSED. The fact was, he'd been thinking for some time of getting out of the barbering business. It didn't pay, never had. He'd gotten into it at the wrong time.

THE BRONZE CHARIOTEER
(GREEK, 478 or 474 b.c.)

The standard dating of course is absurd. Socrates was not born until 470 b. c., so the statue must have been done to commemorate the games of 454 or 450 b. c., at the very latest. By 446 b. c., the date of the next games, Socrates was serving in the military and had long since abandoned his dreams of athletic glory. Indeed, the sculptor-genius whose name is forever lost to us has captured him at the very moment when he realizes that sun-drenched afternoons on the playing fields of Athens are irretrievably behind him and his future belongs to the fallen world of philosophy.

The most dramatic part of the statue, to which our eyes are immediately drawn, is the severed reins. We marvel at the sculptor's sense of timing. To have caught them at the instant they broke (extended straight and taut) would have been absurd; to have them hang down limp would rob the figure (static enough as it is) of tension. Instead, the reins have snapped an instant before and are falling, like Socrates' hopes and dreams.

But the severed reins hold our attention for only a moment. What we ponder endlessly are the eyes, clouded and distant with pain and foresight. We do not have to look at the relaxed hands and arms, the feet planted flat on the ground like slabs of dead meat, the tunic-draped torso and legs as monumental and motionless as a fluted Doric column to know that Socrates will not run off in pursuit of the horses that broke away only a moment before. No, the eyes tell us that he has no hope of retrieving the horses in time for the chariot races, where he thought that his chances of victory were golden. And the eyes know so much more: that he will drop out of the long run from Olympia to Pyrgos, humiliatingly, less than halfway through, near Dios; that he will not return for the third round of the wrestling competition, where he had

seemed to be invincible; that he will not even attend the award-
ing of the laurels but will instead sit in the shade by the stream
and try to mount the ladder of knowledge. At this, too, he will fail.

An all-too-human Socrates, he will react basely at first, accus-
ing Clinias of sabotaging the reins.

"I threw him in the first wrestling match," Socrates fumes, twisting the reins into a Gordian knot. "And then too he was always
jealous of my special friendship with Phaedrus."

But he has already relinquished his anger by the time Polus takes
the reins from him and shows him the ragged ends where the
leather, unaided, had parted.

"Old, worn out," Polus says, trying to be sympathetic but unable to keep a note of exasperation and even something like satis-
faction out of his voice. "You should have checked your equipment.
You've been careless lately, my friend. Too cocky by half. Too much
time off picnicking with Phaedrus. If you want to be champion,
you have to work at it, Socrates. I told you and told you. You should
have checked your equipment."

"There wasn't time," Socrates says lamely, knowing it's a lie.

"Time! Well, you have plenty of time now—four years to make
sure your harness is in shape for the next games."

A vague terror freezes Socrates' heart. He turns from Polus and
tries to calm his breathing. In four years he will be twenty-four
[that is, in 446 b. c., so now we see clearly that the date of the
statue must be 450 b. c.], too old for the games. No one has ever
won an event at twenty-four. The few who tried were pitied,
laughed at.

During the long run from Olympia to Pyrgos the next day
Socrates lopes along in a sort of reverie. He watches the feet of
the runners immediately before him: they seem to be pumping
straight up and down instead of spinning forward in bounding arcs.
Their sweaty thighs and upper arms, instead of swinging back and
forth, seem to flash from light to shade, light to shade in the drowsy
sun. It occurs to Socrates that perhaps the nature of things depends
upon the angle at which we see them. He is not happy with this
possibility.

When he recovers from his reverie he finds that the other runners have left him far behind. He cannot see them, but up ahead,
over the hill, he hears the cheers of people lining the path. By

the time Socrates jogs up among them, they have stopped cheering and are turning for home. They do not cheer, or laugh, but make way and stare, puzzled, at this young man who runs with a look of terror on his face and a set of broken reins draped around his neck.

Near Dios he gives it up, and he does not appear the next day for the semifinals of the wrestling competition. Then, instead of attending the awards ceremony on the last day of the games, he sits by the stream and turns the reins this way and that, contemplating the torn ends from every angle, until finally he concludes that the flaw is not due to treachery or his own carelessness or even the gods but rather to some fundamental imperfection running throughout the fabric of the world.

It is a conclusion he can live with, he decides, only if this is not the only world.

Time passes. He serves honorably in the Persian Wars, marries badly, becomes a teacher. The pay is miserable, but he enjoys, after class, watching the boys play in the field beneath the Acropolis: tumbling, throwing stones, boxing with their tunics wrapped around their fists to forestall broken teeth. In the sun, the sweat on their gleaming bodies is like streaks of gold. There is a truth there that he can't quite plumb. To his students he talks about caves, blinding light, a ladder of knowledge, a world of perfect forms, but in his heart he believes none of it.

The years come and go as, despite his prayers, his wife lives on and he grows old.

To escape his wife and Plato—who tags along after him everywhere, copying down each stray remark—Socrates sneaks off for long walks in the countryside with Phaedrus. They lie hip to hip in the meadow and stare at the clouds as they did when they were lads of ten.

"Does time pass, Phaedrus?" Socrates asks. It is an old question, a joke between them.

"Time passes."

"And what have you learned in your long life, my friend?"

"That 'the due proportion of mind and body is the fairest of all sights to him who has the seeing eye.' I seem to remember that from somewhere. For my eye, though, you can keep the mind as long as the body is fair."

Socrates laughs and slaps Phaedrus' flank.

"And what has been your goal in life, my Phaedrus?"

"An acquired judgment that aims at what is best."

"And what is best?" Socrates muses, as much to himself as to Phaedrus. Then, rolling up on his elbow and staring down at Phaedrus: "Have you ever known the best?"

Phaedrus thinks a moment, grows solemn. His eyes are rheumy, and the last few wisps of hair that cling to his temples are white as snow.

Finally, he says, "Once, on my fourteenth birthday, after years of being afraid even to try, I cleared the wall behind the Minos' cottage in one leap. That, Socrates, was the best."

Socrates kisses Phaedrus' sunken cheek.

"Old friend."

Three days later they find Phaedrus leaning against the door-jamb of his home, gazing with astonishment into the distance: dead.

Socrates' end comes two years later. By then he is weary of theories of government, politics, court intrigues, well-meaning friends, his students' undiscriminating acceptance of all his half-baked ideas, everything. At his trial he refuses to defend himself. Entreaties to escape to a new life in Corinth nauseate him, and he does not reply. In fact, he does not utter a word the last three days of his life until, maddened by Crito's endless tears and "What must we do, Socrates, what must we do?" he reaches down into a black well of cynicism and replies, "We ought to offer a cock to Asclepius. See to it, and don't forget."

What is remarkable in this death scene is not that Plato was able to fashion from these two brief bitter final sentences three grand dialogues but that the sculptor of *The Bronze Charioteer* somehow divined that the posture of the young man's hands holding the broken reins was almost precisely that of the old man holding the cup of hemlock, from which he had drunk a moment before, and that on both occasions the eyes had the same glazed, distant look, the charioteer's clouded by humiliation and the knowledge of loss, the old man's by death and one final memory: a cool breeze, a blue sky, and a green field upon which he would run, throw, catch, tumble, rise, and run, he was then sure, forever.

THE *DAVID* OF MICHELANGELO

1. David

"I know your pride, and the naughtiness of your heart," says Eliab, his brother.

But David is not listening.

"I killed a lion and a bear that stole one of your sheep," he says to Saul, whose eyes already begin to glaze over with wonder and madness. "I chased them down. I hit that bear so hard he dropped the sheep right out of his mouth. The lion came for me, and I grabbed him by the beard. I said, 'Whoa, old fellow!' Then I killed him with one blow."

The circle of warriors tightening around Saul and David push Eliab farther back until soon his mutterings can no longer be heard.

David does not think himself vain. He believes that he has simply told a truth the king will surely be glad to hear.

He does not yet understand the madness in the king's heart.

But David does know that his moment is at hand. After a lion and a bear, a fat Phillistine will make a short morning's work.

(He does not have to go naked into the valley of Elah. He could have worn the brass armor, weighing 2,000 shekels, provided by Saul—could at least have worn his shepherd's smock, his sandals, and his goatskin cap against the sun. But no. He goes naked into the valley, and just before killing the giant he turns back toward Saul and Jonathan and Eliab—his white young manhood shining in the bright morning light like polished stone—and almost smiles. He looks as if he might be posing.)

2. Goliath

He too was a shepherd. On his wild rocky hillside in Gath, he would cradle the little lambs gently against his huge chest and nuzzle his face into their necks and breathe the rich, warm, heady odor of young wool. He would study each newborn lamb, rubbing his chin, until he had thought of a suitable name: Wildflower, Mothersmilk, Raincloud. His tender ankles could only painfully support his bulk, so he could not have pursued a strayed lamb far beyond the slope rising above the hut where he lived with his mother. The sheep seemed to know this and would stay near and always come when he called them by name. When it came time for a sheep to be slaughtered, Goliath would weep. But even this the sheep seemed to understand, and they would turn their necks lovingly toward the knife.

When the king's men came to gather recruits for the war against the Israelites, Goliath's neighbors sent them to him as a joke.

"Go to the hut where the widow lives, at the foot of the rocky slope, and there you will find a giant who will slay all your foes," they said, pushing their beards up to hide their smiles.

"Mama!" he cried.

They pounded his fingers with the butts of their spears to make him release the roof-pole, and it took six of them to load him into a dung cart. No horse could carry him, and they knew that he could not walk all the way back to camp.

He sat weeping and reciting, without hope, the names of his sheep as they hauled him off down the road. His mother wept long after he had passed from sight.

She knew she would never see him, or the dung cart, again.

At the camp of the Phillistines, the training captain would slap Goliath's fat buttocks with the side of his sword and squeeze his huge quivering tits, crooning, "Ooo, baby, ooo, baby, ooo," while Goliath bawled and the men howled their laughter.

In his coat of mail weighing 5,000 shekels, Goliath could not even stand up without help, much less walk from the camp at the top of the hill down into the valley, where he was to shout his challenge to the Israelites. So they built a frame atop a small wheeled platform, all of gopher wood, and tied Goliath upright to the frame, which they concealed as best they could under his long scarlet cloak. Two long ropes were tied to the frame and then passed through the hands of two files of soldiers, whom Goliath seemed to be pulling down the hill after him. It was they, of course, who were letting him roll down slowly to the bottom of the valley, where Goliath stood, a strange, monstrous vision before the Israelites, who cowered before his challenge for forty days.

"The fattest scarecrow in the world," wheezed the general of the Phillistines, holding his sides and laughing to see Goliath pinned to the frame.

Goliath's voice was high and girlish, and he could not have made himself heard to the Israelites, trembling in their camp at his approach, were it not for the dwarf hidden under his cloak, who, at the proper moment, rammed into Goliath's anus the sawed-off end of a shepherd's crook. Goliath would bellow then, yes indeed.

"Send me your champion, that we might fight together!" he would bawl.

"They will never send a champion," the Phillistine general said. "They will cower in their tents a few more nights, then give over all to me."

When Goliath saw the naked boy stride down the hill toward him, he thought of his mother, and of his lambs, and he smiled.

"Shepherd!" he shouted, with no encouragement from the dwarf squatting under his buttocks. And as the boy began to spin the sling faster and faster over his head, Goliath shouted once more, "Savior!"

3. Michelangelo

Michelangelo has caught him in all the arrogance and cruelty of youth.

His left knee is canted delicately forward and in, almost girlishly—this for Jonathan? His left arm curls upward, holding the sling draped over his shoulder loosely, insolently. His right hand hangs heavily at his side, huge, blood-gorged. There the white marble is almost dark with blood. Though the legs, arms, and torso slant languidly this way and that, the head is perfectly erect, his gaze flat and direct, leveled at Saul, who, just across the valley, writhes in an agony of prescience. Saul knows: the old king under the pitiless gaze of the new.

It is not until a moment later, when he turns from Saul, that David first thinks of the giant. David does not think much of him even then. Hasn't he killed a bear with one blow and bearded the lion?

It is strange, though.

A handful of Phillistine soldiers run up behind the giant and seem to give him a shove, then run off up the hill with the rest of their fellows, laughing. The giant seems to glide slowly toward David without moving his arms and legs. He smiles and shouts two words. A Phillistine insult, no doubt.

But David does not think much about this, either, and it is not until after he has cut Goliath down from the wooden frame that it occurs to him to hack off Goliath's head and feed his carcass to the fowls of the air, the beasts of the earth.

* * *

Goliath surely did not know that his part in the divine plan was to grow fat so that one day he could have his head bowled down the valley of Elah for the glory of a minor god, bloody and vengeful, bent on hegemony.

And David—a good man, by all accounts, from then on—did not realize that he was doomed to be frozen in stone at a moment of stupid, ruthless vanity, forever, in the Academia, in Florence.

RUMPLESTILTSKIN

Ruben Silberstein.

That was the name. Not good, not bad, a name, that's all. What can you ask? A little respect. What did I ever get? A boot in the face.

Ru ben Sil ber stein.

I'd say it to them a syllable at a time, singsong like I'm swaying over the Talmud, and these schmucks would come back with

Rum pul stilt skin!

Actually it was worse at first. I shouldn't tell you. All right I'll tell you. *Rumpled foreskin,* that's what he'd call me, Johann, the wheelwright's whelp with his blond hair and eyes grey as the edge of a freshly sharpened ax. The other schmos were too dumb to get the pun, illogical for a foreskinless Jew though it was, too stupid to get their pork-fed tongues around the name, so when they picked up the chant, I was Rumplestiltskin! Rumplestiltskin!

I'd run home with tears salty as blood leaking into my mouth and they'd dance outside the door.

Rumplestiltskin! Rumplestiltskin!

Ruben, you've got to learn to take it, my mother would say. You've got to learn to laugh. Be more like Abe Wallenstein. Laugh a little, Ruben.

Abe Wallenstein. The fat kid whose father brewed the beer and assisted the blacksmith on Herr Mueller's estate, where we, the Silbersteins, lived, my father the carpenter. (Bad profession for a Jew, my father would say. With Joseph and the cross and that whole schmeer the goyim's palms sweat around a Jewish carpenter. Be a blacksmith.) So I was apprenticed to Proel the German—this was when Jews could still join the trades, things got worse for us later. Proel, so dumb he couldn't pour piss out of a boot, and Wallenstein—Abe's father—who could work iron like a sailor works a Dutch whore, but he's a Jew so he assists for twenty years while Proel's the boss.

Be like Abe Wallenstein, Ruben. Laugh a little. Fat Abe would squeal with laughter every time he saw the goy thugs coming. While I'd hide in a bush or run already crying to my momma, Abe would cavort straight for them singing

> Fat Abe Wallen stein,
> Got nothin' in his bean!

> Fat Stein Abe Wallen,
> Look at his pants fallen!

> Fat Wallen Stein Abe,
> Pisses and shits like a howlin' babe!

Abe would do pratfalls into muddy ditches, walk forehead first into linden trees, eat dried birdshit and smack his lips. The goyim loved it. They'd roar with laughter when Abe sat kerplop! in a pile of fresh cowdung, slap him on the back and say, "You ain't bad, Abe, for a Jewboy."

Then one day in December—I forget the year, I think I was eleven then, and fat Abe ten—we were walking arm in arm along the bank of the canal when a gang of goyim sprang out of the woods and began firing rocks at us. While I fell wailing to my knees, covered my head with my arms and called for Joshua to fall ruthlessly among them, Abe picked up a stick and went into his blind man routine, hobbling along tripping over exposed roots and slamming into trees. The goyim stopped throwing rocks and laughed until they grabbed their sides. Abe tottered on the bank, then staggered out onto the ice-covered canal, poking his stick crazily here and there and spinning his feet like the wheels of a runaway dogcart. How they laughed! When the point of Abe's stick went through the ice, and then Abe too, all of him, in a splintering crash that sent the water spraying up in a silver shower, oh what a triumph! When he thrashed up out of the water, grabbing at the crumbling edge of ice, they laughed, and when he screamed "Help me! Help me!" they laughed and skipped rocks across the ice at him until he went back under. It was a very cold day, and it didn't take long for a film of ice to begin forming in the irregular circle where Abe had broken through. The goyim left soon after, and didn't bother me at all. I was very grateful.

Two years after I was apprenticed to Proel the blacksmith, old Herr Mueller died and left the estate to his son with one eye, who promptly kicked all the Jews off his land and burned to the ground the hovels we called homes—to kill the smell of Kike, as he put it. So we moved to the city, Vien, where we lived the six of us with another family of seven in one dark room that smelled of smoke and baby shit and death sweats.

I loved it. I could go for weeks in the ghetto and never see a goy. When I was ganged up on and beaten for being a new boy who wouldn't laugh or join in their childish games, it was Jewish fists that brought the blood, and if someone cried, Help me! Help me!, heads turned, and hands lifted, and help was given.

Peace to all that!

The only cloud in my sky was my little brother, Samuel—bless his soul! curse his tongue!—who brought the *name* with him. One day in pique or sport he danced after me in the street and sang, Rumplestiltskin! Rumplestiltskin!, and so I was once more, thereafter, forevermore.

My father wanted me to enter a new blacksmith apprenticeship, but I had no money for the fee, so I wandered the streets doing an occasional odd job—shoveling manure from the stables of Simon Salt, the richest Jew in the ghetto, or carrying water at a pfennig a bucket for fat widows—or pilfering fruit from the wagon of blind Saul, who would send curses shrieking after me as I raced away down the street: May you marry a sow and dine on your children! Steal from a poor blind man. May the rats eat your cock!

Mostly I walked and walked so that fatigue would kill my hunger. It never did.

I was sixteen when I fell in with the alchemists. Not the old men of lore, with long white beards and blazing red eyes and black cloaks, but bright young men who in a better time would be professors at Heidelberg or Bologna. We talked about turning base metals into gold, sure, but that was just a means to a greater end, a method of financing our studies into the way things worked and what things are, really *are*, what makes a thing one thing and not another, one man a Jew and not another—but, well, peace, peace to that.

I listened and looked and studied until by the time I was twenty I had learned all that their simple arts could teach, and then I went out on my own. I shut myself away from men, in the ghetto still, but easy enough to do even there, always too easy for me to do. I rarely saw my family, I forgot my few friends, I went days at a time without speaking to another soul, I forgot to eat until I grew dizzy and weak. I did nothing but study things in their essence, what made them what they were and what they were not. Finally, I learned to do what the others could not. Transform! Lead to gold, iron to gold, stone to gold, wood to gold, cabbage to gold!

I became wealthy, right? Wrong, wrong. It was hard work, the chemicals costly, and in the end you cleared enough to keep the wolf from the door—but he stayed across the street and licked his chops.

I was in my early thirties, I think—somewhere I lost track of the years—when the story flashed through the ghetto of the poor peasant girl who had been ordered by the king to spin straw into gold—or die.

Thank God it's not one of ours, I heard a Rabbi say. We've had all the abuse one people can bear. Let the Christians butcher their own.

I spat at the Rabbi's feet, and then raced through the ghetto until I was out among the goyim. Only then did I stop and ask myself why I was so moved by this girl's plight. I had no answer, except in my mind's eye I'd see fat Abe Wallenstein disappear beneath the cold water, and me cowering on the bank. This time, perhaps, I could help. Jew, goy, did it matter?

It was dark by the time I reached the castle. Legend will tell you that I appeared through the wall or descended from the night air or arose from the black depths, but I made my way through the gates and into the straw-piled spinning room by a more perfect magic: I greased the guards' palms with coin.

She sat trembling at the foot of the spinning wheel.

I cannot do what they ask, she wept.

I can, I said.

I have nothing to pay you, she said, looking at my hooked nose, my squinty eyes. So. She has to put it in Jew terms, I thought.

I can get it for you wholesale. Have to make a sale to the first customer of the day. You know them all. *I* know them all, damn sure.
You have to pay me something, I said out of pure black spite,
then was immediately sorry. The poor guinea brat—obviously part
of the recent wave of unemployed from the depressed Milano
region—had probably never *seen* a Jew before. But it was too late
to back down. She already was raising her sun-browned, calloused
peasant's hands to her neck, from which hung on a frayed string
a crude crucifix carved from a bit of bone. I almost wept.

According to the tale the next morning the king found the room
piled high with gold. Don't believe it. Make it two, maybe three
ounces, Troy. Even a Jew alchemist can't do miracles with straw.
Iron or lead, I'd have done better.

Was the king pleased? Is the Pope Catholic? Straw he's got by
the barn. Gold he can always use a few more ounces of. I didn't
have to be there to figure that one out.

And it didn't surprise anyone the next day when the king went
into the same shtick again: more straw, more gold, or the business end of a halberd. Sleepy and hungry as I was—hard work,
believe it—I hadn't bothered to wander far from the castle. When
the story spread about the miracle of the night before and the
king's latest threat, I was right back at the castle gates. Night falls,
palms open, coins deposited, gates and doors open.

What can you pay me, I said. I don't know why. I wanted nothing, payment enough to put one over on the king, but I already
felt myself part of the myth, the ritual, beyond helping.

A bit of scarf, holey, blue, sweat-stained and reeking of garlic.
Do us both a favor, I said. Tomorrow, when the king pulls this
shit again, make him promise to marry you. I need my sleep. . . .
So he's a king? You're not bad, believe me. A little weak in the
ankles and narrow through the hips, but some goyim go for that.

There was twice as much straw in the room. I worked my butt
off and by morning had a lump of gold the size of the Pope's nose.
I drug myself out of the castle and collapsed in a nearby park.
When I awoke the sun was almost down again, a pigeon had
crapped in my beard, and the fishwives were wetting their pants
over the king's promise—to marry the girl if she spins gold one
more time.

I hauled my aching ass back to the castle. I almost passed out when the guard, well-bribed, unlocked the door to the spinning room. Oi vey! Piled to the ceiling with straw! Barely room for the spinning wheel and the girl.

Guard! I called. A shilling for you to haul this stuff out of here.

The girl let out a wail. I pressed a dozen gold coins—my life savings!—into her hand.

Give this to the king, I said. What does he care? If you've got the magic to spin gold, you've got the magic to stamp it with the face of the sovereign. He won't turn it down, believe me. Besides, I can't face another night of this damn transforming, transforming, transforming. I've got a tension headache and my hemorrhoids are killing me. Too much sitting.

What can I pay you? she asked. My sandals?

She took them off and held them up. I resisted the urge to hold my nose.

Sandals I've got, I said.

My dress? she asked. She stepped out of it like the moon from a running cloud. Her white breasts. Her strong young thighs. My thirty years' virginity, a waste of study and persecution. I felt my strength returning, quite localized.

My dress? she asked again as I gaped and struggled to find my voice.

I don't wear them, I finally managed.

Then what—? she started to say, but then sensed my problem, her solution. Wise child.

She lifted her eyes to heaven and sighed, then shrugged and spread her dress on the cold, bare stone floor. The shiksa lay back, spread her legs, and beckoned.

That night, between white goy thighs, the silver moon peeping through the barred window, Ruben Silberstein spun gold until the dawn!

* * *

So that was it. Love?—naw!—who am I kidding? She wasn't as innocent as she looked. Dumb as I was I could tell I wasn't her first. That night she traded for my gold, I think, the thing of least value to her. She put her hands behind her head and dozed while I ground away. And to tell the truth, after three or four times it got pretty mechanical for me, too, but I figured, what the hell, may never get another chance so I'd better take advantage.

A month later the king and the girl got married. No smirking on my part. We each of us got what we wanted. No losers. I went back to my studies, planned a trip to Amsterdam where I heard some young Polish emigre was doing interesting things with water-based solvents. When the news spread a short time later that the bride was showing, I didn't even pay any attention. I had problems of my own. My poor old mother died of consumption. Today I can't think of her without tearing my beard and weeping. My father fell from the roof of a house where he was patching shingles and cracked his spine. He lay in bed like a sack of rotting turnips and begged for someone who loved him to push a good sharp knife into his heart. My sister, thirteen, they caught in the hay with the pock-faced baker.

She married the baker, and I took care of Papa.

When the church bells rang out the birth of the prince, I shrugged and scratched my father's ear who couldn't raise a hand. But then the snickering rumors started. Count the days, I heard them say. I counted. Then I thought. Then I knew.

I got the widow next door to watch Papa. She'd rifle the pantry, but a fair price—we all have to live.

They were all new faces among the castle guard, but their palms opened and closed just as easily. The queen grabbed the edge of a gilded vanity and swayed, face chalk-white, when she saw me.

I just want to see the child, I said.

He sleeps, she said.

I won't wake him, I said. One look.

Never!

Just one look, all I ask, no more. One look at my son.

Never, not ever! Filthy Jew! Kike! Get out before I have your head served to the pigs!

Tears blinded me. Hot bile rose in my throat and I could hardly speak.

Don't call me that, don't call me that! I whimpered like a child, full of self-loathing at my weakness.

Kike! she spat again.

You'd better call me by my name, I warned, unable to get the childish whine out of my voice.

Three days, I said, I give you three days to call me by my name or or...or I'll use all my powers on the boy.

My powers? What was I going to do, turn his little pecker into a lead sinker to scare the fishes with? All my powers? Still, my past performances transforming the straw and the tales of Jew devilment that goyim scare their children with scarred her face with fear, and as I backed out of the room and rushed down the vaulted hallway of the castle I heard her break down in sobs.

So. You know the rest. Or a doctored version, anyway. How did it go? A fairy godmother? or birds flitting through the kingdom to find the hunchbacked gold-spinner's name? I'm five-nine and erect, even after all the years of desk work. And *birds* was it? Birds shmerds. The goyim knew the universal magic as well as I. They flashed gold. No surprise. I expected it. *Wanted* it. Wanted to hear my name on the queen's lips, lips that I'd kissed one blessed night of a cursed life, the name that should have been my son's. Ruben Silberstein.

Rumplestiltskin! Rumplestiltskin! she said, laughing her horsey Wop laugh, and I screamed No! No! and stamped my foot, catching my heel on the gilded, eagle-claw leg of the queen's vanity chair, and I heard a bone in my ankle snap.

Before I could limp out of the queen's boudoir, weeping and cursing, I was caught by a passing palace guard, unbribed. The king stormed in, my son clutched tight in his arms. Hair hers, eyes hers, lips hers, nose mine! The king looked at her, looked at him, looked at me, and knew. A man who knows his noses.

I was held up against the wall, my robes opened. The king's knife was sharp and sudden. Such a little thing I asked of the wench his wife, and what he took from me. You should be grateful, they tell me. He spared your life.

Grateful.

* * *

At home I would wave the flies from my father's face and pick fleas from his beard.

Let's curse God and die, my son, he said one day.

God? I said. When's the last time you saw his face around here? You want to know whose stick stirs the pot, go find the man with the gold.

Since my father's death I live in the country, back where I

started. I avoid at all times the company of women. I sleep in a hut of stone, mud, and thatch. It is bitter cold winters. I live on nuts and berries, sometimes a rabbit. I do not observe the dietary laws. At night, occasionally, I search for the mandrake root, thought by some to have magical powers, but I no longer study transformation. I do not believe that things can be transformed. Things are what they are: stones, metals, people.

I take no consolation in such knowledge.

CONCH SOUP

Every day except Sunday, at ten and two o'clock Ernie Barto would drive the old converted school bus over to the Jumbo Gumbo on Decatur between Iberville and Bienville to pick up the widows and retired school teachers and the occasional family from Wisconsin for their forty-five minute "Chartreuse Line" tour of the French Quarter. The entire "line" consisted of the one bedraggled bus repainted a cheap chartreuse enamel that had flaked in many places to reveal the yellow and black beneath. Lou Bedrosian, the owner, had somehow jerryrigged a window air conditioner to run off the battery. It sat on the floor against the back door of the bus. Anyone within ten rows of it would get off the bus with his legs aching from the cold, but Ernie, Delia Martin, the tour guide, and those sitting at the front of the bus didn't feel a thing. None of the used batteries Lou bought for the bus lasted more than a month, but that didn't bother Lou. Used batteries were ten bucks apiece while a whole new air conditioning system would set him back over two thousand. You figure it, Lou would say.

"So we're a little seedy," Lou would shrug on the rare occasions when Ernie suggested that he fix up the bus. "You telling me that *New Orleans* ain't seedy, for Chrissake? Seedy is colorful. The tourists love it."

And, in fact, despite everything the tourists did seem to enjoy themselves. Delia Martin was an interesting guide, and hardly ever did a tour pass without one or more of the tourists "oooing" and "aahing" over Ernie's handling of the bus in the narrow streets of the Quarter.

After picking up the tourists in front of the Jumbo Gumbo, Ernie would follow Decatur to Canal Street, then turn and stop in front of the Marriott to pick up Delia. That was where her brother-in-law dropped her off every morning before the ten o'clock tour. It didn't strike Ernie as strange that he would leave her at the Marriott rather than the Jumbo Gumbo. He couldn't imagine Delia at the Jumbo Gumbo or, indeed, many of the places whose sordid histories she revealed in her remarks on the tour. Delia was what Ernie thought of as a "lady." Her clothes were expensive if not quite of the latest fashion, and there was never a hair or a pin out of place. Ernie assumed that she conducted the tours as a hobby. She lived with her sister and brother-in-law, not quite in the Garden District, she assured Ernie, but "near it. They're quite kind to me, Odette and Kenneth."

"An old maid," Lou snickered behind his hand to Ernie. "You pop that one and the sonic boom'll break windows for miles around."

Delia was in her early to mid-forties—ten to fifteen years older than Ernie—not exactly old maid age, and she was a pretty woman. Still, Ernie had to admit there was something vaguely spinsterish about her. She was always polite to Ernie, outwardly friendly, in fact, but he sensed she was relieved when the few opportunities for them to talk to one another on the tour were past. Once after the ten o'clock tour was over, just to be friendly Ernie asked Delia if she'd like to have a cold drink with him, and she'd fluttered like a cornered bird, "Why no, why no, I just couldn't." And only when he'd turned to walk away did she recover herself enough to call after him, "Oh, but I do thank you. You're so kind."

About once a week Lou would tease him about Delia, even though he knew that Ernie was recently widowed: "Hey, you ought to try that out, Ernie. She'd think it was her last chance and give it all she's got. Turn you every which way but loose, guarantee it."

It was the sort of comment that you'd expect from Lou, a cynical Armenian from Brooklyn who claimed to have moved to New Orleans because he heard they spoke Brooklynese there. "What a fucking joke. You people don't talk *nothing* like Brooklyn. You go to Brooklyn and talk like that, they'll laugh you off the goddamn street, guaranteed."

Lou's rationale for moving to New Orleans made no sense to Ernie, but then Ernie never could figure out much about Lou. Like where he got his money. He had a house over on Esplanade with a double gate opening onto a courtyard large enough for Ernie to park the bus in after each shift. Not the choicest area of New Orleans to be sure, but, still, it had to cost him a bundle, and the tour couldn't possibly bring in much money.

What puzzled Ernie most, though, was why Lou stayed in New Orleans, which he held in withering contempt.

"Know what I ate today down at the Jumbo Gumbo?" Lou asked one day, leaning against the fender of the bus, which Lou had just parked in the courtyard. When he stood up, a baseball-sized flake of chartreuse enamel came loose and stuck to his elbow. "Conch soup. You eat that stuff?"

"Don't think I've ever had it."

"Lived in No all your life and never ate conch soup?"

One of the things that Lou hated about New Orleans was the way the natives pronounced the name: *Nahlens.* He called it N. O. at first, which later became "No" and sometimes "the Big No" in sardonic rebuttal of "the Big Easy."

"Conch soup isn't New Orleans, Lou. It's Caribbean, I think. Jamaica or Bahamas, maybe."

"Ha! Don't tell me. That stuff is pure No. You know how they make it? They take this big goddamn snail or something and pull its insides out, then chop it up, guts and brains and asshole and all, and make soup out of it. At least that's what they start with. They wind up throwing everything they got in there, garbage and all, I know that, they ain't put anything over on me. Then they expect you to eat it and *like* it, *pay* for it. That's No for you. Don't tell me that's not the Big No."

"Why do you live here, then? Why don't you go back to goddamn picturesque Brooklyn?"

Lou ignored him. You couldn't talk to Lou. You couldn't tell him anything. Like the chartreuse paint on the school bus. Lou wanted Delia to start off the tour by talking about the color, how it was part of the New Orleans heritage—the one contribution of African slaves to the architecture and design of the deep South.

"It's good luck—wards off evil spirits, or some doggone thing," he concluded. (Ernie watched his language when talking with Delia.)

Delia tried to explain to him that he was right in general about the color, but not about *that* color, the color he'd chosen for the bus. That was a harsher, darker color, nearly a green. She offered to take him over to St. Peter to see the house that was painted entirely in the good luck color of the African slaves, but Lou refused, almost lost his temper.

"I spent tweny-two dollars to get that paint mixed, and I ain't about to change it. It's close enough for me, and it'll be close enough for these schmucks. What do they expect for seven-fifty?"

"Well, I just can't tell them something that's not true," Delia said flatly.

Lou and Ernie had been surprised by Delia's resolute stand, and Lou backed off. They compromised: Delia would begin the tour with a joke about the bus being a Yankee's idea of what the African chartreuse looked like; then she'd point out the genuine thing on St. Peter.

"Can't insult me by calling me a Yankee," Lou shrugged. "My eyes fill with tears of gratitude."

After picking up Delia at the Marriott, Ernie would turn down Bourbon to Galatoire's, where Delia would begin her comments. During his first couple of weeks on the job, Ernie had been so intent on handling the bus in the narrow streets that he had paid little attention to what Delia was saying, but gradually he became more confident at the wheel, and he began to listen. He found it fascinating. He knew nothing about the history of his own city, he realized. He had hated the French Quarter, would never go near it if he didn't have to, until he got the job driving for Lou. But now he was beginning to almost like the Quarter and his job, too. Most of it, that is.

It wasn't until the last stage of the route, after they'd worked their way to the Ursuline Convent on the northeast end of the Quarter and turned back south on Decatur, that Ernie would begin to grow nervous. Frequently Delia would have to tell him to slow down as he accelerated past the French Market. More than once he sped on by the Jackson Brewery without giving Delia a chance to mention it to the tourists. By the time he turned up St. Louis for a final loop into the Quarter before coming back down Conti to Decatur a block and a half from the Jumbo Gumbo, he could hardly control himself, much less the bus. Once he'd gone up over the curb, scattering a group of schoolchildren. When he pulled the bus up before the Napolean House at St. Louis and Chartres, Ernie would grip the wheel and stare at the amoeba-shaped darkening on the pavement—there, always there—two paces out from the sidewalk, directly across from the No Parking sign. He would become nauseous. He would try not to weep.

But, after all, this was what he'd come for. The job had been an excuse to bring him into the Quarter, which he had loathed, so that he could stare at the spot where his wife had her throat cut by Charlie Guyon.

* * *

When he was twenty-four, Ernie had gotten bored driving a delivery truck for a lumber yard, so he joined the navy to see the world. In three years he never got farther from New Orleans than Mobile, Alabama, where he was a clerk in the naval recruiting station, and where he met Darlene. Darlene said she'd do anything to get out of Mobile, even marry Ernie and move to New Orleans.

Four years later she ran off with Lon Watts. Like Ernie, Lon drove a Dixie Beer truck, and Ernie had thought they were good friends.

On the day that Darlene walked out on him, Ernie returned home from work to find the house just as he'd left it that morning. There was no note, everything was in place, he couldn't tell that she had taken anything. From all appearances she might just have walked down to the corner store. But he knew she was gone, gone for good. She didn't call him until a week later.

"You're a nice guy, Ernie, but I want more than you have it in you to give—more in every way."

"I understand," he'd said, holding tight to the receiver with both hands.

He didn't understand anything. He didn't know what "more" meant, and he didn't know what "in every way" meant. The only thing he understood was that she was gone, but in a sense he couldn't believe that either. He'd walk around in a daze. It was kind of like after a hurricane had hit, and people would stare around themselves, knowing that sooner or later they'd go back to doing what they'd always done, but not just yet. Not just yet.

He hadn't recovered—hadn't even *begun* to recover—from Darlene leaving him when the police called him in the middle of the night to tell him that she had been murdered on St. Louis, right in front of the Napolean House. She'd gotten into a fight with her boyfriend, and he'd chased her into the street—or she chased him into the street, it wasn't clear which—and cut her throat.

Ernie thought that by "boyfriend" they meant Lon Watts, and he vowed to take his revenge, but when he was at the city morgue identifying the body he learned that the murderer's name was Charlie Guyon. Lon called him the next day when he heard about it. Darlene had left him after only a couple of weeks, started living with this Guyon fellow in an apartment in the Quarter. Lon sounded bitter.

Things would have been simpler if it'd been Lon who did it. Ernie would have bought a gun, found Lon, and shot him. Then the police could have done what they wanted to with Ernie, but at least it would all have added up somehow. But this Charlie Guyon. This apartment in the Quarter. Everything was at a wrong angle, Ernie couldn't make sense of it.

After the funeral, Ernie never went back to work, so he lost his job. He took to walking the streets and riding the street cars from one end of the city to the other, hours at a time. One day he found himself in the Quarter, on St. Louis, in front of the Napolean House, staring at a discoloration on the pavement. It wasn't red or even a dirty rust like dried blood—it was more like a perpetual shadow—so it couldn't be what Ernie was thinking. He was being foolish. It was probably just an oil stain.

But he couldn't take his eyes off of it. He stood in the sun, staring, until a black man with a strange accent, who evidently worked in one of the buildings nearby, came up to him.

"Yah, mon, dat where it hoppen. Right der she bleed to death, mon. I seen it all. She chase dis fella out into de street der, and when he pull out dat knife, she jus raise she chin up an smile a big smile at him, smile like a woman do when she in love. Den he cut she throat. Bleed, oh mon, bleed. Rain don't wash dat away, no mon. Dat *passion* blood."

Ernie came back to the Napolean House every day after that, sometimes spending hours staring at the spot, watching it change color as the sun rose and then fell over the Quarter. Often he would not think of Darlene or what had happened there but would think only of the spot itself, as if to understand it was to understand everything. But each time he saw it was like the first time—it was like the day he'd returned to that empty house, like the telephone call a week later from Darlene, like the call in the night from the police.

He would see the black man often, and for a while they would stop and talk, but later the black man began to avoid him.

One day Ernie offered to buy the black man a beer, but the man waved him away. "No, mon, you got something domn bad, and if it be catchin', I don't want it."

* * *

One Wednesday afternoon Lou climbed aboard the bus after Ernie had let the passengers off at the Jumbo Gumbo. On the drive back to the Marriott, Lou outlined for Ernie and Delia his plan for adding a night run to the tour, starting at eight o'clock and emphasizing the night life of the Quarter. Ernie was agreeable—he could use the extra money Lou promised—but Delia was hesitant. She didn't like being in the Quarter after dark, and night life was a bit beyond her field of expertise. Lou begged her just to try it once or twice—on Saturday nights at first—to see how it went over. Besides, he'd already had circulars printed up and distributed to the souvenir shops and cheap hotels and motels where the "Chartreuse Line" got most of its customers.

"And the truth is, Delia, I need to generate some cash."

In that case, she could hardly refuse to try it once or twice, she said.

Ernie showed up at Lou's place on Esplanade that Saturday night at seven-thirty. He had a key to the padlocked gate, and usually he let himself in, but tonight he wanted to make sure he saw Lou. Lou hadn't paid him that afternoon, as he usually did. He said from now on he'd pay him when he came to pick up the bus for the night shift. It was a cash-flow issue, Lou said.

There was no answer at the door. The house was dark. Ernie went around to the side and unlocked the gates, and the bus was not in the courtyard. He peered through the side door of the house but could see nothing.

Ernie knew he would never see Lou Bedrosian again just as surely as he had known Darlene had left him that day he returned to an empty house.

He walked on up Esplanade and turned down Bourbon and wandered into the Quarter. It was early, but already the street was thick with tourists. Pitchmen swung open doors of bars as he passed to reveal strippers grinding away on bartops and in gilded cages, spread-legged on velvet swings.

He had just entered a bar to get a beer when he remembered that Delia would be waiting at the Marriott. He left the bar and walked on down Bourbon to Canal Street. Delia, just inside the glass doors of the Marriott's lobby, came out, worry and surprise on her face, when she saw him walking up.

He explained what had happened.

"Ernie, there has to be some logical explanation for all this."

He shrugged.

"Did you check at the Jumbo Gumbo?"

Ernie said he hadn't.

"Perhaps, we should do that. Maybe Lou was having something repaired on the bus, and he got back home too late, so he drove it over to the Jumbo Gumbo himself."

"Well, maybe. . ."

Ernie had been prepared to tell Delia that Lou was just gone, that's it, forget about it, but she seemed so upset that he was afraid she'd start crying.

They decided to walk down to the Jumbo Gumbo. It was dark by then, and there were few people on the streets in that part of the Quarter. Delia moved closer to him as they walked, and he resisted an urge to take her by the arm. He could think of nothing to say.

At the Jumbo Gumbo, the owner, whom Ernie knew only as "Mr. Jim," laughed bitterly when Ernie asked about Lou.

"When you find him, Ernie, you come tell me, OK? Because Lou's into me for a little bit, too—just a little bit."

Delia didn't seem as upset as Ernie had expected. In fact, she seemed to want to cheer *him* up.

"Well, there are worse things than losing a job, aren't there Ernie? We'll both land on our feet, I feel certain of it."

"Sure."

He couldn't think of what else to say, so he asked if he could buy her a drink and was surprised when she said yes. They sat at a table near the window, and Ernie drank a beer and Delia a glass of white wine. Then Delia said she'd been so nervous about the night tour that she hadn't eaten dinner. Ernie said he wouldn't mind a little something himself. He picked indifferently at an oyster poorboy while Delia ate the special for that night, conch soup, which she said she'd never had before. It was different, she said. She couldn't say if she liked it or didn't like it, but, "Nothing ventured, nothing gained." Remembering Lou's description of how conch soup was made, Ernie declined Delia's invitation to sample it.

Ernie had another beer and Delia another glass of white wine, even though she said she just never, ever had more than one. He watched her hands flutter like frightened little birds about the tall, thin-stemmed wine glass. He resisted an urge to reach over and take her hands, press them together, calm them before they blundered into the glass.

Delia was talking as if she were afraid to stop. He'd never heard her talk so much—not that he was really listening. Mostly he nursed his beer, rolling the mug slowly back and forth between his palms, and thought about how his life had gone to hell. First losing Darlene, then his job. You couldn't compare losing a job to losing your wife, of course, but there was a pattern there that bothered him. He should have been able to read the signs, should have seen it all coming. He'd never trusted Lou, had he? The money business—where it came from, how he could afford the big house on Esplanade—had always been a mystery. Ernie shouldn't have been surprised at what happened with Lou, nor with Darlene, for that matter.

Now that he looked back, yes, there had been signs, long before that phone call a week after she left him, when it was too late: "more than you have in you to give," she'd said. What in the hell did that mean? He suddenly recalled how she used to look at him a certain way, there toward the end, taking ferocious puffs on her cigarette, almost as if she hated him. But the look wasn't hatred. What was it? And in the last few months before she left, their lovemaking—well, she'd gotten colder somehow, she was sort of *absent.* He hadn't thought about it much at the time—that was just what happened after you'd been married a while, he'd assumed—but now he saw it as one of those signs he should have been able to read. How much had he failed to read, to see? Was the problem with *him?* He was damned if he could see what he'd done wrong. Sometimes things just didn't work out, that was all.

Ernie looked up from his beer. Delia had stopped talking, paused as if to give Ernie an opportunity to say something. Say what, though? He started to smile but then stopped. Although he hadn't been listening closely, he had the impression that Delia had touched on some less happy subject.

He cleared his throat and said, "Yes, well, sometimes things just don't work out the way you'd think. You get caught off guard."

"That's it, Ernie, that's it exactly. Who would have expected it? He was still a young man after all—still in his mid-forties. We just couldn't abandon him to a nursing home. Odette and I knew instinctively that I'd be the one who'd take care of him while she'd have the husband, even though I was the older sister. Looking at us, most people think Odette's older, but that's not the case. . ."

Delia paused and lowered her eyes and smiled. Once more she seemed to be expecting Ernie to say something. He took a long drink of beer. Her smile faded. Her hands fluttered about the glass, landed on it, raised it almost to her lips, then she put it down and sighed.

"Sometimes I feel that I'm a walking cliché—the long-suffering, self-sacrificing Southern Belle. Melanie Wilkes or a character out of Faulkner."

"Blanche DuBois," he offered.

Delia blushed.

"I don't read Mr. Williams. A bit sordid for my tastes."

How could a New Orlean tour guide not read Tennessee Williams, Ernie started to ask, but he wasn't interested enough to pursue it. Instead, he ordered another beer. Delia declined a third glass of wine, and Ernie thought that signaled the end of their evening, but Delia started to talk again. Talked about caring for her father, about taking correspondence courses to keep her mind sharp. He died, she moved in with Odette and Kenneth. She described what she did with her day—volunteer work, watercolor lessons—described her room right down to the doilies she'd crocheted herself, the paintings of Audubon Park in all four seasons she herself had painted, the lace canopy over her bed in lilac, the lilac bedspread, the violet satin pillow in the shape of a heart that Kenneth and Odette had brought back from their honeymoon in Martinique. On it was stitched in bright pink, AMOR TOUJOURS.

"It wasn't meant to be a sort of joke, if that's what you're thinking," she said. "Kenneth and Odette aren't like that."

Ernie took a drink of beer.

His mind wandered again. He thought about what he'd do if he found Lou. He'd work him over. Not kill him, but work him over good, give him something to take back to Brooklyn.

He tried to imagine what he'd do if he found Darlene. But then, what was he thinking? She was dead, gone. He'd never see her again. But if he could, though, what would he say to her? He'd say, let's go back to just the way it was. We'll pretend nothing happened. Everything will be the same.

Suddenly, Ernie was stunned by the horrible possibility that Darlene wouldn't agree to the deal. She'd choose Lon Watts, choose Charlie Guyon. She'd choose death.

And then once more Ernie saw that look on Darlene's face— almost tearing at the cigarette, glaring at him with something like hatred, but not hatred, yes, there it was: boredom and disappointment.

". . .more than you have in you. . ."

"I gave it my best," Ernie heard himself saying.

Delia stared at him a moment, bemused, then her look softened. She reached over and patted his hand.

"I know you did, Ernie, I know. None of it's your fault. It was Lou. You're the kindest man."

She paused once more and looked at him tenderly.

"May I tell you a secret, Ernie? May I? That time you asked me out on a date, it was the first time I'd been asked out since Daddy's stroke. It was so kind of you, and I think of that moment often." She gave his hand a little squeeze. "Often."

With something like panic Ernie tried to think what she could be talking about. Was she insane? Then he remembered the day months before when he asked her if she'd like to have a cool drink with him after the tour. Could that have been the "date" she was talking about?

Gently, he tried to extract his hand from hers, but Delia held fast.

* * *

Outside the Jumbo Gumbo it was Delia who suggested they walk around the Quarter a bit, and it was she who took his hand and led him down Decatur.

They found themselves following in the wake of some sort of parade that was banging and crashing its way toward Jackson Square. Delia seemed content to keep on the same course, to catch up with the revelers, even, but Ernie guided her off onto a darker, quieter side street. Only after they'd walked on for half a block did he realize that they were on St. Louis and were coming up on the Napolean House. He wanted to turn back but suddenly was out of breath, dizzy. He grabbed the pole of a No Parking sign and tried to steady himself.

"What is it?" Delia asked.

"Here—" was all he could get out.

"Here? . . .Oh, yes! I see," she said, almost laughing. "All right, if you insist."

She took a couple of steps out into the street, then turned back toward him—toward the Napolean House—swept her arm in an arc before her and began to intone:

"And here we have the Napolean House. Our ancestors built the house in response to the rumor that Napolean was to escape from St. Helena and sail to New Orleans, which would become the seat of his new empire. The people thought that with Napolean would come resurrection and transformation, that the filth and disease and squalor of the Louisiana swamps would magically take on the grandeur of Paris and the splendor of Versailles. But that did not happen, of course. Napolean was condemned to die on St. Helena, just as we are condemned to live in New Orleans."

Delia covered her mouth and giggled like a schoolgirl.

"I always wanted to do that—couldn't you just see the look on their faces? Aren't I terrible, though! People think I'm such a stuffy old goody two-shoes, but if they only knew. . . . Ernie? Are you all right? Ernie?"

"There—"

He pointed past her to the spot, the stain, on the pavement.

"What?"

"There. The spot. See it?"

"What spot? I see nothing."

Delia looked this way and that for a moment, then stopped, put her hands on her hips, and shook her head. She walked back over to Ernie, took his arm, and stroked it.

"Ernie, you naughty, naughty boy. You've been drinking too

much, haven't you? And on an empty stomach. You hardly touched your sandwich tonight. You just need something to eat. Come along now, Ernie. Come along."

"No, I—"

He gestured once more toward the spot, but Delia caught his hand like she'd catch a butterfly—so gently—and drew it to her breast.

"*No,* Ernie. You come with me."

* * *

Holding cans of beer, glasses of wine, or mixed drinks in their hands and laughing hugely, tourists squeezed past Ernie and Delia on the congested sidewalk.

They were in a long line of some sort. But a line for what? Where? Ernie's mind didn't seem to be working right. Maybe he had drunk too much. Then he recognized where they were. The first stop on the tour: Galatoire's.

Delia was beaming. A fine sheen of perspiration glistened across her forehead, and her eyes shone.

"Oh, Ernie, I've always wanted to go to Galatoire's. Can you believe I've lived in New Orleans all my life and have never been to Galatoire's? How I've dreamed of coming her with my beau, my man."

She pressed his arm to her.

Ernie wanted to run, but he was hemmed in by the crowd.

"It's just a dream come true for me. Have you ever had a dream come true, Ernie?" she asked, looking up into his eyes.

He looked away.

"No. I didn't need to dream. I had everything I wanted."

"Oh. That must be nice—to have everything you want," she said. But she didn't say it like she thought it was so nice.

She started to say something else but then stopped and looked up toward the entrance to Galatoire's. She seemed to be straining to hear something. The others around them had hushed and were listening, too.

Then Ernie heard it: the faint sound of glass breaking in the distance. It grew louder. No, not breaking, but glass tinkling. Glass against glass. It swept up the line of revelers toward Ernie and Delia. And then he understood what it was.

All up and down the street people with drinks in their hands were clinking glass against glass, rings against glass, glasses against windows, against street signs, against the windshields of slowly passing cars. Everyone was tinkling glasses and straining on tiptoe to see the tuxedoed groom and white-gowned bride, standing at the edge of the street just outside the door of Galatoire's. The tinkling noise rose in a crescendo until the groom turned the bride to him and kissed her, then the mob let out a cheer and applauded.

Then, quietly at first, but quickly growing louder and more frenzied, the tinkling started up again. It was all around them, the tinkling, the celebrants pausing only long enough to kiss their partners. Ringing, tinkling, kissing.

Delia stared up at Ernie and smiled. She reached up and put her hands around his neck. He tried to pull back, but her clasp was like iron. She drew his face down toward hers. The light from the streetlamps leaped and danced in her eyes. Her breath smelled like conch soup.

SOMETIMES I WONDER

I had been gazing sorrowfully at the grey hairs curling over my thin wrist when she passed by my table. Our eyes met for the briefest moment, before she moved on. I resisted the urge to turn and watch her as she left the restaurant. There would have been no point in it.

I was disturbed and strangely moved. I knew that we had never known one another, had never even met, but I sensed that we had seen each other, once, long ago.

I lifted the coffee cup toward my lips. It was almost full, very hot, and my hand trembled—call it by its name: palsy. I leaned forward to meet the cup. Then I stopped. I remembered where I had seen her.

It was forty years ago—almost exactly!—August 28, 1947, the Stars on the Water Ballroom, which had begun as a roadside tavern and then grew into a small dancehall during the Depression. Not long after the Army Air Corps base opened during the early years of the war, it expanded again, became a ballroom extending from the dusty parking lot out across pilings beneath which lake waters lapped in soft counterpoint to the rhythms of Miller, Goodman, the Count and the Duke above. Its glory years immediately followed the war. The young men returning home could not get enough of dancing, dancing, and there were crowds every night, on the weekends spilling out into the parking lot where couples danced close and slow, dust rising about them in a pink and blue mist, lit by the neon sign over the entrance: STARS ON THE WATER.

I saw her—we saw each other—on a Saturday night, just before the ballroom closed. It would have been 12:50, 12:55. The bandleader had announced the last song, "Stardust." The dense and ebullient crowd from earlier in the evening had thinned to a last few melancholy couples who moved easily into one another's arms and began to sway.

I was alone. Maybe I had come with friends. We had probably drunk cheap bourbon, made passes, been rebuffed. The friends had left. I had remained. Why? I don't know. Much of the evening has been lost to me, but I remember *her.*

She was alone. Or maybe she was with friends. She stood with two or three friends. She sat with a friend on one of the long benches that smelled vaguely of lake water and were worn smooth by years of young lovers pressed thigh to thigh.

I stood not ten feet away leaning against the frame of the French doors opening onto the narrow porch that skirted the ballroom on three sides. I watched the dancers for one last moment, then turned to leave, and in turning I saw her. We looked into each other's eyes.

We held each other's gaze for one second, two seconds. Then—timid or haughty or tired, I don't know why—I looked away and left the ballroom.

I looked away!

One more second and she would have ducked her head shyly, but not before I caught her smiling. I would have crossed over, awkward and nervous but trying to appear as jaunty and debonair as Fred Astaire, and said, "I think there's enough stardust left for one more turn about the floor. . ." And we would have danced, me stiff-kneed and gangling, palms sweating on her palm and back, she turning her face down into my breast, suppressing a smile as her friend on the bench grinned and winked and waved with a flutter of her fingers.

When that last dance ended, I would have let her disappear into the night without so much as asking her name. All that week I would have been in an ecstacy of joy and hope and doubt, and when I had stood hour after lonely hour in the ballroom shadows that next Saturday night as she did *not* come, I would have thought how sweet it would be to let myself down into the cold dark lake waters, to drown away my agonies among the pilings that pulsed to the lapping waves, the lulling music.

She would not have come on the next Saturday either, or on the one after that, and I would have descended into a paralyzing melancholy, then bitterness, then the mask of indifference.

I would have stayed away from the ballroom on the fourth Saturday night, going bowling with friends instead, and I would have laughed and swilled beer and celebrated freeing myself from a childish spell until the crashing pins roared like the collapse of a vacuous world.

And I would have rushed back to the ballroom, midnight on the stroke, and she would have stood there, lonely and desolate until she saw my face, then she would not have been able to help smiling in relief and love. I would have taken her hand and led her out onto the porch, the stars winking off the purple water beneath us, and turned her face up to mine and kissed her gently.

We would have been married in the Wesley Methodist Church on June 18, 1948, a grey humid day. She would have wept as her father led her down the aisle, but at the reception in the basement—white cake with white icing, pink punch, assorted nuts, pink, yellow, green and white mints—she would have laughed and glowed and I would not have been able to take my eyes off her.

We would have driven to Kansas City to the Muelebach Hotel for our honeymoon. I would have been clumsy the first night. She would have winced and pulled away, crossing her hands over her groin and weeping, and I would have said, almost crying myself, "I'm sorry I'm sorry! We just won't do it then. We'll never do it if you don't want to."

Of course we would have "done it" many times after that, but she'd never have seemed to want to.

It would have been two days before I would have gotten around to washing the car, and the HOT SPRINGS TONIGHT Andy Herman wrote on the trunk in orange-tinted egg whites would leave a stain that would never come entirely clean. When I would have finally traded the old Chevy in on a new Pontiac Fire Chief six years later, the salesman would have leaned down and, frowning quizzically, traced the ghostly letters on the trunk until his finger suddenly stopped, and he would have looked up with a grin of complicity.

By then I would have finished medical school—not pharmacy school, for her I would not have settled for being a pharmacist!— at the University of Missouri and would have set up a practice in Columbia. Little Jimmy would have been two years old by then.

She would have doted on him, taken him to bridge and garden club meetings, he would have ridden along in the golf cart at the country club, gone everywhere dangling from her hip until he was four, five, his feet hanging down to her knees, and she'd have to list awkwardly to the right as she walked and would have developed back trouble by the time she was thirty.

I would have massaged her back, gently kneading the flesh around the vertebrae, working my way slowly down until I would have kissed her buttocks, which she would have clenched, rolling away and throwing the covers over herself.

It would have been a Tuesday night in October of 1964 that she would have pushed me away and said, "Don't touch me. I'm sorry, but I don't want you to ever touch me again," and I would have spent the rest of the night sitting stiffly in the expensive Queen Anne wing chair, staring blackly at the Hummel on the butler's table: round-cheeked girl straining on tiptoe to kiss blushing round-cheeked boy.

Two days later by chance I would have seen her pull in to the parking lot of the Holiday Inn on Providence Road, walk up to a second-floor room hand in hand with a tall blond man younger than she. He would have squeezed her bottom with his left hand as he ushered her into the room, and she would have flashed a wild and happy grin, lacerating my heart.

"And you would never move your hips for me! Not once!" I would have hissed from behind the tree across the parking lot, pressing my head so hard against the bark that for days the impression would remain.

I would have loved her so terribly, even then, and I think she would have loved me. We would not have been able to talk, that would have been it, nor touch one another, really touch, except in dancing. If we could have danced "Stardust" forever. . .

Only then, when I found that I was losing her, would I have begun to think of Jimmy. I would have realized that I could not lose Jimmy because I had never had him. With long hours at the office and hospital and volunteer work at the Rural Health Center clinic, I would have had no time for him on workdays. On weekends I would have allotted him exactly thirty minutes, and I would have watched the clock closely.

Once, I would have walked into the house and seen him sitting on the couch, and he would have said, "Hi, Dad," and for two or three desperate seconds I would not have been able to remember his name.

Sometime around his junior or senior year he would have begun to be seen in Nehru jackets and opaque granny glasses and would whisper among his friends of Haight-Ashbury, capital of a country utterly foreign to me.

I would have been a naive physician, missing all the signs of drug use in my son until one of his teachers would have called, saying, "I think we have a problem with Jimmy." I would have thanked her profusely for her concern while secretly dismissing her as officious.

Jimmy would have flunked out of the University of Missouri in his freshman year, dropped out of William Jewell the next, then volunteered for the Marines as the U.S. involvement in the war was winding down, but still in time to die among elephant grass, Quang Nam province, September 3, 1971.

I would have grieved for Jimmy. Who would have thought it? But, yes, I would have grieved.

By then she would have been years beyond her affairs with young blond gods, and we would have drawn closer again, sharing grief and guilt and degeneration. She would have begun to put on weight, and even by then my right hand would have begun to shake with palsy, forcing me out of the operating room. Arthritis would have settled into her back, my hip.

It would have taken her almost ten months to die of cancer. There would have been one week, maybe two, during her slide from plump to cadaverous that she would have hovered at about her weight when we first met. She would have worn a wig of long auburn hair, and her eyes would have shone with—pain, of course, but what one could have sworn was love.

She would have been beautiful, and one spring night at an outdoor concert on Francis Quadrangle we would have held each other and danced slowly in and out of the ruined columns to the tune of "Stardust," while her strength lasted.

In her pain near the end she would have begged for death, and on her last day her pupils would have contracted to pinpoints and she would not have known or heard me when I asked her to forgive me everything.

She would have died leaving me unforgiven, an aging bachelor, palsied and arthritic at sixty, closing down my pharmacy each night to sit alone in some cafe, watching the women pass, saying to myself, "Were you the one?" or "Was it you?" until my coffee grows cold.

I, IN RENOIR'S *LA BALANÇOIRE*

"*Merde!*" he groans, slamming down his palette as I emerge from behind the tree once more.

Babette—or so I call her; I don't know her name—sighs in exasperation, releases the rope with her right hand to wipe the perspiration off her forehead and almost loses her balance, glares at me. She seems on the verge of tears. I feel sorry for her. She has been on the swing—*la balançoire*—all morning as the master—the great Renoir—awaits just the right moment—fleeting and eternal—to record his impression. I have not helped in this regard, I admit—this is my third intrusion—but it is so little that I ask.

"Monsieur Renoir," I plead, stepping back so that only my head peeks around the tree, "*un momento* of your time, *por favor*—uh, that is, *s'il vous plait.*"

In one sentence I dispose of all my French and Spanish (I was drafted before I got to the foreign languages in college), then blush violently at the snickering of the shy little girl (left edge of the canvas) who insists on keeping the tree between me and her.

"*Imbecile!* Go! Go!" Renoir shouts, hunching his shoulder in a furious gesture meant to accompany the "Go!" that comprises, apparently, all his English. The gesture would be more forceful if he would join it with a waving of the hand, a shaking of the fist, but he has taken up the palette once more and, despite his annoyance, is swirling together reds, yellows, and even a bit of blue in an attempt to capture the peculiar shade of my blush. "Bah!" he shouts and shakes the palette knife at me. Bits of pigment fly off. Too much or too little of something, it has come out blood red.

"Go!"

---

*   *   *

"Come on, come on, time to go. Come on, Denny," Szkotak says, shaking me. "Don't want to keep Mr. Charles waiting."

Szkotak has just come back from midnight chow at the mess hall. I can smell the powdered eggs on him. He is sitting on his cot, leaning over to shake me. Evidently he thinks I have been asleep. Perhaps from where he sits he can't tell that I have my head hanging over the opposite side of the cot just enough to see the book, opened on the floor almost exactly in the middle, to plate 115. Surely, though, he sees the beam of the flashlight that I hold in my left hand.

"Charley's going to have to dance alone tonight," I say. "I'm not going."

He's heard it before, we all have. We'd all heard it and said it and meant it—meant it with all our hearts—but after saying it we'd get up and put our boots on and take our M-16s out into the night where, most nights, nothing at all would happen.

I heard Szkotak stand up behind me and begin to shuffle away.

"Well, you can lay here and sleep all night if you want to, but I'm going out and have myself some fun," he says. Then, slapping me on the heel as he moves past the end of my cot: "Come on. Time to mount up."

"I'm not going."

*   *   *

"Go! Go!" the other one says—Pierre I call him. He seems even angrier than Renoir. Perhaps he's paid a flat fee for his modeling, which he had imagined would be a fast job, but now with this boorish American's meddling. . .

Probably Pierre does not speak English at all but is merely parroting his master, so that his command comes out "Guh! Guh!"

He brings his arm up and cocks his fist menacingly.

"Hit me if you want," I say, overwhelmed with sadness. "All I wanted was to be a part of this moment—"

—of this exquisite moment, in the little park near the Moulin de la Galette, Paris, 1876, late spring, with the sun brilliant, broken into dazzling whites and blues on the pathways swept by the long ladies' gowns then in fashion—

"—this moment forever. . ."

118

Pierre senses my sadness, or perhaps he is intimidated by my size—a good head taller than he—or my scruffy beard, which I had grown specifically for Manet's *Dejeuner sur l'Herbe (Sketch)*, plate 55, but left when I found the shadows at right-center and far right too dark and forbidding, the grass too thick, causing me to neglect the picnic I had crashed and concentrate instead on looking for trip-wires, toe-poppers, and bouncing Bettys. Or perhaps Pierre is embarrassed by his own ridiculous appearance in the little-girl bonnet with the brim turned up in back and decorated with the precious little blue bow, which, surely, no self-respecting Frenchman could ever have worn.

Whatever the reason, Pierre turns away from me in confusion, faces Babette, his left hand thrust down casually into his trouser pocket but his right hand still raised and curled into a fist, now impotent and absurd.

"Just let me stay a few minutes," I say, trying to keep a quiver of desperation—so out of keeping with the mood of the day—out of my voice, "let me stay forever. After the sitting, we'll go to a little sidewalk cafe. I'll buy us all a glass of cool white wine. We'll be friends. Friends? *Ami? Ami!* We'll be *amis!*"

"*Amis?*" Renoir says, looking up from his canvas. "*Amis?* Ha! Idiot!"

* * *

"Vannatta, you miserable idiot, you poor excuse for a human being, get your funky tail off that cot! It's time to kill people, boy! Move!... Are you deaf on top of impotent and stupid? Get your worthless behind off that flea-ridden cot, get your distinguished weapon, and get your posterior *moving,* four-eyes!"

"No," I say to Sergeant Jessup, a teetotaling, Bible-reading Baptist from Arkansas who daily invents new ways to curse us without taking the Lord's name in vain, "I'm not going out there any more."

Sergeant Jessup steps quickly around the cot and takes a soccer-style kick at the book, but I'm ready for that and jerk it up out of his way and roll over onto my back. I fumble the book and lose my place, open it to Sisley's *Misty Morning,* plate 139, a cool country I had visited often before—

"You know what you are, Vannatta? You're nothing but a gutless coward, that's all. That's the whole yellow-tinted story."

—especially in the dry season. We were up in the Central Highlands then, and the sun was so hot. You could not bear to look at the sun or touch anything that the sun touched. Especially then I loved to walk among the yellow and pink and white flowers, the long dewy grasses of Sisley's morning, but I could not stay long. The bamboo fence running across the background was unsettling. The strangely Oriental tree writhing on the upper right of the canvas, the old woman falling to her knees at the first *whump!* of the mortars, the smoke rolling in from the left, all seemed manifestations of some shadowy land of the dead. And in the Central Highlands, I did not need another land of the dead.

So I thumb back toward Renoir, pausing over Pissarro and Monet on my way to plate 115, as Sergeant Jessup prances about my cot, clenching and unclenching his hands as if it is all he can do to keep them from around my neck, reviling me, calling me a coward, a deadbeat, a coward, a malingerer, a coward coward coward.

I cant the flashlight to catch blues such as were never seen in the sky over Vietnam, and admit everything.

*   *   *

"I admit I have no right here," I say, "but, let's face it, if you folks had taken care of business at Dien Bien Phu, I'd be back in the world, back in Missouri, right now and we'd all be a lot happier."

Renoir shrugs almost imperceptively.

He lays his palette and brush down and moves up behind Pierre, takes him by the shoulders and moves him over beside or slightly behind the swing (to your right). Pierre holds both hands out as if reaching for or just releasing Babette, who raises herself up on tiptoe and leans forward slightly—an unnatural position it seems to me, almost as if she were falling off the swing. When he has finished with Babette and Pierre, Renoir steps over to the little girl and positions her (seated, her skirts concealing her pudgy knees) at the base of the tree. The little girl raises her hands toward Babette as if to clap or plead, "Take me, take me, Mama!"

This, in fact, is the position I had found the group in—Renoir at his easel—when I made my first intrusion. And it's now clear what Renoir's new tack is—to ignore me, to continue to work as if all that existed in his world, his moment, were sunlight, trees,

a gay young couple with their little girl, and *une balançoire*.
But it's no good. Oh, he tries. He dabs at the canvas, smiles, cocks
an eye up at the sun, whistles and hums, then gives up the charade, slams his palette down and clasps his forehead in his huge
right hand, clenching his eyes as if he has such a pain.

I feel sorry for him. Into his perfect day has stepped this grimy,
bearded (the CO had exempted me from shaving for two weeks
because of a terrible skin rash) stranger in camouflage fatigues
(in my haste I'd forgotten to change), which has thrown everything off. What's more, we are no longer alone. Five others have
now invaded our section of the park and are chatting on the path
at the upper right corner of the canvas. This, surely, has totally
upset Renoir's calculations.

"Look, Mr. Renoir," I say, "you need me now. Those five people
have thrown the whole composition off. Without me, your composition will lack balance."

In my desperation, I may have hit upon a truth. It's obvious he'd
intended the man and the woman on the right to be balanced by
the child and the great bulk of the tree which occupies the whole
side of the canvas on the left. But now with five additional people
encroaching on the right, the whole thing seems to, well, list so
to speak.

I try to communicate my theory to Renoir, who obviously doesn't
understand my words but just as obviously is following my
gestures, is weighing Pierre, Babette, the child, the five figures at
a distance, me.

"What you need, Auguste," I point out cheerfully, "is another
warm body."

* * *

"Warm bodies, Vannatta, we need more warm bodies out there
for a little S & D party," Lieutenant Maguire says, slapping me on
the back good-naturedly. (I had rolled back onto my stomach after
Sergeant Jessup left, the book on the floor, my head and the hand
holding the flashlight over the side of the cot.)

I flip through the book, mull over Degas's *Melancholy,* his bloody
Mme. Camus with a Japanese Screen, shudder, turn back to plate 115.

"I'm not going out anymore, Lieutenant."

"I know, I know," he says, resting a hand on my shoulder in a fatherly gesture. My sweat rises under his hot palm. "None of us want to go out anymore. But that's just it, isn't? None of us want to go, but we can't all just quit, can we? If even one of us pulls out, it hurts the whole team, it hurts everybody's chances, isn't that right?"

Lieutenant Maquire is a tall blond Georgian, second year law student at Georgetown, sharp. Favors the rational, humanistic approach. He played basketball at Georgia Tech, likes to "play some hoop" with the brothers, likes to think of himself as well-liked by the men, basically just one of the boys. We hate him. Worse than Jessup, worse than Top, worse than the CO. He's not a dumb-ass lifer like them. He's sharp, should know better. But, no, he's a team player. He wants the team to win.

He launches into a lecture about how my rifle squad won't be as effective without me, and if the rifle squad isn't as effective, the platoon isn't as effective, and then everybody is in danger. I almost say that all he's worried about is the paperwork for the court-martial if I refuse to go out, but I don't. I know that's not true. Maquire believes what he says, and maybe he's right. That's why we hate him.

"I'm not going out."

Maguire takes his hand off my shoulder. I can hear him breathing. I can hear the men outside the tent, moving slowly, talking softly. It is so peaceful.

Finally, Maguire says, "I think it's going to be bad out there tonight, Vannatta. I think we're going to lose somebody tonight. I can feel it, you know?"

I don't say anything.

"Remember when we lost Kreppfle? He didn't want to go out either, but he went. Remember Kreppfle?"

"Yeh, I remember Kreppfle."

"Remember Brader? Got wasted when we were up in the Highlands, remember?"

"I remember Brader."

"He was a real pain in the ass. Hated the army. Hated the war. Bellyached about everything. But he went."

I don't say anything.

He sits there the longest time. Then he sighs and stands up. He seems about to move off when he stops and bends down and takes the book and turns it so he can see the cover.

"Phoebe Pool. *Impressionism*. Oh yes. I love the Impressionists, too. My favorite was always Renoir."

He leaves and I train the flashlight on plate 115. The blues, the whites, the spots of yellow are swimming, blurred. I wipe at my eyes.

I remember Kreppfle. I remember Brader.

* * *

Renoir, clearly disconcerted, looks to Pierre and Babette for help, but they turn away from me, embarrassed. Renoir hesitates a moment, then comes over to me, takes from somewhere inside his jacket a soiled silk handkerchief and hands it to me and—as I wipe at my eyes—puts his arm around my shoulder and hugs me. Softly he speaks to me, comforting, incomprehensible phrases.

I hiccup, blow my nose, and offer back the handkerchief. He gestures for me to keep it.

"Just a corner of your moment, forever. All I ask," I say.

He can't understand the words, but he understands something. He considers me for a moment, glances at Pierre, Babette, the little girl, the five people stalled on the path a dozen steps away. *"Oui.* OK."

He positions us about the swing, repositions us, puts us back where we were, adjusts Babette's hands on the ropes, turns Pierre's head a certain way, seems satisfied, then changes everything. Suddenly, he begins to paint. The brush and palette knife fly across the canvas with miraculous speed. In a flash—a moment—it's over.

"Alors. . ." he shrugs, nods at the canvas, turns and walks a few steps away as if now indifferent to all that has transpired.

Babette, Pierre and I run to the canvas. I am filled with great joy, great sadness. Never was a path so dazzling in the sun, never was a dress so white, never a shade so cool. But Babette—weary after hours on the swing—has not been able to hold her pose. Renoir has caught her just as she slumped to the left, her hip pressing against the rope, her head resting on her left hand, her smile faded to a grimace, her eyes slanted off to some distant sorrow, perhaps thinking of her boyish husband (not Pierre), who died five years before in the defense of Paris. And in the finished painting Pierre does not face the viewer as originally planned but stands with his handsome profile half-hidden beneath the "bonnet," the absurd little ribbon dangling down his neck. His left hand is in his pocket, his right raised and clenched, but not as if in a fist. Rather, it's as if with trembling hand he's about to extend a finger for each of his dead sons: one, Pierre, Jr., who died on January 12, 1898, beaten to death by a fellow army officer after a bitter argument over Zola's *"J'Accuse"*; two, Henri, who died later that same year, the exact date of which authorities were never able to supply the distraught father, of sunstroke on the aborted march to Fashoda; three, Lucien, who rose to the rank of colonel before being among the first to drown in mustard gas, July 17, 1917, at Ypres. (The French say *eepr,* the English *wipers;* let's compromise, call it *weepers.*) The little girl stands to Pierre's left, still keeping the tree between her and me. She is heartbreakingly serene and innocent. Renoir has lightened her hair to almost an auburn, has softened her Jewish features, has allowed her eyes to be weighted with no foreknowledge of the gates that will close behind her, forever, at Dachau, November 3, 1943. And me? Renoir has solved the problem of my vilely mottled camouflage fatigues by placing me behind the tree with just my face peeking out. On my head he's painted a straw bowler in place of my olive-drab army cap. My eyes are still red from crying. Altogether, though, I look the happiest one there.

I cross over to Renoir, who remains turned away from the canvas. I want to apologize for intruding on his moment, for causing him to warp the tree trunk unnaturally to hold the oval of my face—to apologize for everything. Struggling with my poor French, though, in trying to say "I'm sorry," instead I say *"Merci."*

Indeed, the broken light on the path, the blues, the whites, the shimmering spots of gold, Babette's glorious dress—it is enough, enough for all of us. Babette and Pierre, the little girl, we all gather round the great Renoir.

"Merci," we all say in chorus, *"Merci."*

Unable to maintain his pose of indifference, Pierre breaks into a smile and nods happily, acknowledging our praise.

But then the moment is passed.

They all turn and look at me expectantly. Renoir cocks an eyebrow, waiting. I smile sadly, wearily.

"Yes, it's time. OK, mount up!"

Renoir folds his easel and lays it across his shoulders, arms raised and hands draped over the frame. He moves off up the path, slowly, steadily, one foot in front of the other, trying not to count the days, counting the days. Pierre follows, stepping gingerly, peering nervously about his feet for trip-wires, even though we're not yet out of the fire base. Babette hikes the little girl up on her hip and moves off with the desperate resignation of refugees everywhere. I sling my M-16 over my shoulder and bring up the rear. We pass through the concertina-wire-strung entrance of the fire base, move on past the guarding bunker.

From the blackness of the bunker I recognize Wilson's voice, from second platoon: "Hey, Vannatta, kill a couple of Slopes for me!"

'You got it, bro!" I say, pumping my fist.

Then, with the slow, steady, weary tread of veterans, we move off up the trail.

A VETERAN OF THE WAR

The Vietnam war had been a big disappointment to Walt.

He had come near to volunteering for the Marine Corps. He had imagined returning from the war and walking the halls of Central High in dress whites with bands of ribbons across his chest. Several times over the winter and spring of '69 he'd gone down to Second Street on a Saturday and walked back and forth in front of the Marine Corps recruiting station. He never went in, but once the recruiting officer came to the door and stood with his hands on his hips, glowering at Walt.

"You got what it takes, boy?"

Walt had been caught off guard, and he hurriedly turned and walked the other way. When he was almost to the corner of Louisiana, he whirled and said, "Yeah, I got what it takes."

But by then the recruiting officer had gone back inside.

He received his draft notice in April, and at 8:00 a.m. on June 10 he and forty or so other draftees gathered at the train station for the three-hour trip to the induction center in Memphis. Vera Wilson, the Selective Service Director for Pulaski County, walked around with a clipboard checking off names and ignoring a greying woman who supported herself with one hand against the wall and sobbed,

"I bet her son never got drafted! I bet her son ain't going to Vietnam!"

Walt wouldn't let his mother come down to the train station with him. He hadn't even told her about being drafted until the night before. He didn't want her to worry. When he told her, she didn't say anything, just held on tight with both hands to the edge of the kitchen table.

"Don't worry, Mom, I'll make it back OK," he said. "I'll keep my head down."

His father hadn't said anything either, which didn't surprise Walt since by then he was into his eighth or ninth beer. After six he would just sit and nurse his grudge against MoPac, from which he had retired on partial disability before the age of forty.

"I need a volunteer to be team leader for the trip to Memphis," Mrs. Wilson called out. "It'll go right down in your record. Look good. Get your service career off to a good start." She looked directly at Walt, then away, and pointed to a college boy in black horned-rim glasses who shrugged sadly when she said, "You."

On the train, Walt was drinking orange vodka with a freckle-faced boy from over around Lonoke when the "team leader" came down the aisle toward them. Walt resisted an urge to hide the bottle between his legs and said, "Watch me pop ol' college boy between the eyes." But all the college boy did was to ease into the seat beside them and, grinning sheepishly, help himself to a drink of vodka. All three had begun to feel a warm glow by the time the train swept into the rice-lands of eastern Arkansas.

"Vietnam," said the college boy, pointing to the rice paddies slipping by the window. "That's where I'll lose my ass."

He brought the bottle to his mouth and tilted it way up.

At the induction center in Memphis the Marine Corps recruiter asked for volunteers and when he got none lined up the inductees along one long pale green wall and walked down the rank pulling out every sixth man. He missed Walt by one, grabbed the fat boy standing next to him by the shirt front and jerked him out of line, saying, "San Diego for you, lard butt." When the fat boy began to cry, Walt snickered with the rest but was somehow uneasy at how relieved he felt to sign the papers that said he was officially in the United States Army.

The new recruits left at 10:00 o'clock that same night aboard a Greyhound bus and arrived at Ft. Leonard Wood, Missouri, sometime around three in the morning, lined up outside a yellowish wooden building and ducked rocks tossed over the roof by another group of inductees, mostly black, from Chicago. The country boy from Lonoke looked puzzled, worried. "You mean we got to be in the same army with *niggers?* I shore never expected this."

Walt scored best in his basic training company on the PCPT test, missing a perfect 500 points only because they teamed him in the 150-yard man-carry with a long-legged oaf whose feet dragged on the ground as Walt ran with him, wheezing and cursing.

"You finished second for trainee of the cycle," his drill sergeant told him, and Walt felt good about it but wished he had something in writing that he could show around in Little Rock.

He almost volunteered for airborne.

He was one of fourteen men in the company who didn't get orders for infantry school at Ft. Polk or artillery school at Ft. Sill. Instead, as the others loaded up in deuce-and-a-halfs for a ride to the air field, Walt took a taxi the half-mile to clerk school, then was sent to Ft. Riley, Kansas, where he worked as an assistant to the OIC of the post gymnasium for twenty months, hitchhiking back to Little Rock when his enlistment was up.

He wore his dress greens and carried his duffle-bag over his shoulder. Older men picked him up and told him stories about World War II and Korea, and he told them about how he'd been in Vietnam for a year before serving out the last months of his hitch at Ft. Riley, and how they could win the war in two weeks if the politicians would just let them fight, and it took him only eight hours to get back to Little Rock.

* * *

He told his mother that he hadn't written from Vietnam because the mail was heavily censored, and he didn't want some college boy ROTC Second Looey reading his personal letters to family. The excuse wasn't really necessary because his mother hadn't written either. She was good as gold—he would fight anybody who said different—but she'd dropped out of school after the sixth grade and now could sign her name only with solemn and pained deliberation.

His father had met him at the door with a big embarrassed grin and raised his arm as if to put it around Walt's shoulder, but then let it drop.

He insisted that Walt take a beer, wouldn't even let him get his uniform off, and they sat side by side on the sofa in the living room, staring blankly at a "Partridge Family" rerun.

His father grinned and shook his head and ran a hand through his thinning hair. Finally he managed to say, "Boy, that must have been something over there."

"Well, there was some good times and some bad."

His father shook his head again and took a long drink of beer and grinned at the TV.

"Yessir," he said, "that sure must have been something."

* * *

The next morning Walt sat out on the front porch wearing his field jacket. By the time the mailman arrived, the sun was high and sweat had turned the collar of the field jacket almost black. Walt pulled the zipper all the way up.

"Damn," he said to the mailman. "I can't get used to the cold. Back in Nam, by this time of day it'd be a hundred and twenty degrees and a hundred, hundred and ten percent humidity."

The mailman bent over and let what looked to be an advertising circular fall through the slot in the door. Then he stood up and said, "Well, I've got a nephew over there right now, and he says they get steak and chocolate milk every night and quarter beer, and he hasn't heard a shot fired in anger in the seven months he's been there."

"Well, he must be in a different place than I was, I can tell you that," Walt said, his voice rising.

He went into the house and slammed the door, then stood in the dim, cool entryway, trembling. He felt like going after that mailman and punching his smug face for him.

But he didn't, and after that he didn't wear his field jacket anymore, either.

* * *

On Friday of his first week home, Walt went down to the state unemployment office on Asher and filled out the forms for unemployment benefits. After he finished, he waited until his number was called, then sat down at a desk before a balding man wearing wire-rim glasses. The man shuffled through the forms for a couple of minutes.

Then he set the forms down, smiled at Walt, and said, "So. Out of the army and now you want a little rocking-chair money."

Walt felt his face grow red and his scalp constrict around his skull.

"Why you dried-up old son-of-a-bitch." Walt could hardly get the words out. "I dodge sniper fire and booby-traps for twelve months in the Delta, come home with an ass full of shrapnel...Why, last week I had to take a damn taxi home my legs hurt so bad. And you begrudge me? ...Son-of-a-bitch."

The man backed away from the desk, pulled his glasses off and rubbed at them desperately with a handkerchief, white as a flag of surrender.

* * *

They usually held the Hardiman family reunion around the 4th of July, but Walt's mother said they'd hold it earlier this year, in June, to celebrate his safe return from the war.

"And we'd hold it right here in Little Rock again, except Hugh'd probably have a hissy over it," she said.

They'd held the reunion in Little Rock's War Memorial Park every year until Walt was a teenager, but then they'd moved it to Malvern because his uncle Hugh complained that War Memorial was getting overrun with niggers.

"Now Rita," his father said. "No use starting something with Hugh. Malvern's a good place."

His father liked going to Malvern. He'd been raised on a farm in Garland County not far from there, and he would say that his life as good as ended when he set foot on the MoPac yard in North Little Rock. "Look what they done to me," he'd say.

Truth be known, Walt's mother liked having the reunion in Malvern, too. It was generally the only time all year she got outside of Pulaski County. Besides, when they held the reunions in Little Rock, she'd worry herself sick for at least a week before. "What if it rains," she'd say. "We'll have that whole outfit right here in this little house. Where would we put everybody?"

Walt didn't care where they held it. He'd always hated the things anyway, had refused to go for the last few years. But he thought he'd go to this one. The uppity Hardiman bunch from Texarkana would probably be there with that uppity girl, Diane, who had been a cheerleader at Texas High. She was a year or two older than Walt and had always ignored him. Maybe she'd take some notice now. He wouldn't mind getting her off into the bushes for a little R & R.

And he made a mental note to tell his uncle Hugh about the nigger who'd saved his life in Nam, when he got cut off from the platoon during a firefight.

*   *   *

Walt didn't volunteer much. Even when somebody finally noticed his slight limp and asked him about it, he just shrugged and said, "Lots of guys came back with a lot worse."

The Texarkana Hardimans had pulled into Waterworks Park in Malvern not long after Walt and his parents, and he noticed right off that Diane wasn't with them. That threw him into a blue funk, and he didn't say much of anything unless someone asked him a direct question.

He started to warm up to things a bit, though, after his mother brought him over a plate of fried chicken and potato salad and baked beans. His cousin Cal brought him a beer, which he solemnly poured out onto the ground. Everyone stopped talking and stared at him.

He smiled sadly and said, "I always like to offer the first one to the guys who didn't make it back."

He began to feel pretty good. Still, he didn't tell any of the stories he'd planned on, not even the one about the nigger saving his life. He'd been just on the verge of it after Hugh Hardiman sat down next to him, but at the last second he remembered the black buck sergeant in Headquarters Company at Ft. Riley who was always on his case about his boots. So he told Hugh about how niggers got away with everything in the army, wouldn't shave, turned up their stereos loud enough to make you cry, and they wouldn't fight. Once the firing started the niggers would bury their heads and let the white boys do the fighting every time. In fact, he'd never seen a white boy from north of the Mason-Dixon line do much fighting either. Arkansas, Alabama, Tennessee. They were the ones that carried the load.

"Mississippi," Walt mused. "I never had much respect for somebody from Mississippi until I got in the army, but let me tell you—those boys will fight."

Uncle Hugh put his arm around Walt and left it there for the longest time.

Walt kept to the picnic table where he ate his lunch. He either sat or stood by the table, staying on the concrete base that the table rested upon. Only once did he leave the table, to look at Robbie Hardiman's new Pontiac Firebird, and then he stepped carefully, almost timidly, with his eyes always on the ground before him.

When he got back to the table, he sighed and ran the back of his hand across his forehead.

"I guess I'll always be a fool about that," he said to no one in particular. "Just can't stand to walk on grass anymore. Weeds?—forget weeds. I'm not getting near them. If you'd spent twelve months watching where you put your foot every single step—toe-poppers, bouncing Bettys—forget it, I don't want to talk about it. I'm sticking to paved surfaces from now on, that's all."

It was the middle of the afternoon before Walt noticed Chub Williams, whose mother was a Hardiman, standing off to the side, staring at him with the strangest smile on his face. Walt started to wave, but stopped and dropped his hand, knocking an empty beer bottle spinning across the table.

What Walt had suddenly remembered was that Chub Williams had been drafted a year before him, had gone to infantry school and then to Vietnam, where, someone reported, he'd gone through hell.

* * *

Every few steps Chub would turn back and motion Walt to follow. It seemed like they had been following the trail for an hour, but Walt knew they couldn't be more than a hundred yards into the woods east of the park, for he could still hear the sounds of children's voices quite distinctly behind them.

Finally, where the trail opened up beside a fallen hickory tree, Chub stopped and squatted down. Walt hesitated, then sat on the hickory trunk. Chub looked up at him and grinned, then looked down, almost shyly, and drew a circle in the dust between his feet with his index finger. His finger moved faster and faster, flew round and round, and the circle grew and grew, then contracted to a point.

Chub looked up at Walt and said, "I know your secret."

Walt tried to smile, but he realized that he had no idea what his face was doing. He might have been smiling or grimacing or crying. He had no idea.

"I know," Chub said again. "I was there, you know. Vietnam."

Walt tried to say something, but couldn't. He tried to swallow.

"Back there—" Chub jerked his shoulder back down the trail toward the park and shook his head sadly—'that was all bullshit. I know."

Then he looked straight into Walt's eyes and said, "You loved it, didn't you—Vietnam. You loved Vietnam. I know, I was there. Hell, people said it was lousy. What do they know? We know. Bottle of coke. That what they called it where you were? Bottle of coke—H. Horse. Smack. Best stuff in the world. We'd come back from a little walk in the woods—you know what I mean—lay down a ten-dollar bill for one of them little bottles, little vials. Bottle of coke. Make the world go away. Here—shit—the world. Hell, man, they can keep the fucking world!"

Chub reared up, stared around wildly, then relaxed and squatted back down.

"Hell, man, I'd go back in a minute. One day—Christmas day, I think!—we were up on a little hill, outside this village that'd given us some trouble, and we called down Willy Pete and popped a bottle. Colors! It was the most beautiful goddamn thing you ever saw. Hell, I've got to get back there. . . . Hey, tell me about where you were."

"Well—" Walt coughed two or three times, studied he back of his hand. "There was this firefight once—bad—"

"Yeh yeh," Chub broke in, nodding and laughing. "Lot of fun! Here. Try some of this."

Chub fished a rumpled cigarette out of his shirt pocket, lit it, and handed it over to Walt. Walt held it in his trembling fingers and smelled the sweet smoke. He'd been a juicer at Ft. Riley, had steered clear of the dopers, two or three Vietnam vets among them. He'd been vaguely afraid of them.

He held the cigarette, Chub staring at him expectantly. Then he put the cigarette to his lips and took a pull. Chub nodded in drowsy contentment.

Chub took the cigarette back from Walt and was about to take a hit when he stopped.

"Hey, I didn't tell you," he said. "I got a Bronze Star! Can you imagine that? For the life of me I can't remember what I got it for. I would've thought that I'd've got a Purple Heart, but they didn't give me one of those. But, hey, who cares? Man, that bottle of coke though. Great times. Once. . ."

Chub's eyes were yellow. His face was yellow. A network of wrinkles like a river delta spread from the corners of his eyes across his temples. Except for that though his face was smooth, virtually wrinkleless. His skin was like yellow butter, oozing sweat.

Walt stared into Chub's yellow eyes and listened to him croon his song of love.

* * *

Walt started, lurched up from the hickory trunk. How long how he been sitting there?

Chub was gone.

Walt could tell from the slant of the shadows that it was much later in the afternoon, but he wasn't sure how long he'd been out there, cut off.

He was dizzy, as if he had suddenly awakened from a deep but troubling sleep. For a wild moment he could not remember which way to take the trail. He listened, but could hear no voices.

He didn't panic. He took several deep breaths to calm himself. Down the hill. Yes, he was sure down the hill was the direction to take.

He started off down the trail, carefully placing one foot in front of the other. He was on his guard now. He would always be on his guard.

DEATH OF A
CASUAL ACQUAINTANCE

Something must be wrong with the Wilson family. They have taken the death of Archy Norton, a mere acquaintance, much too hard.

Bill Wilson, the father, has taken the news the hardest, or so it seems. He laughs when he hears the news. "Laughs," we say, but we need a better word for the dry, hollow, bone-white sound that he coughs out as if in stunned pain.

"Impossible! Ha!" he "laughs" and shakes his head.

It is lunchtime of the day before Christmas when his wife, Peggy, finally breaks the news to him. She'd heard about it from Alissa Lipsmeier hours before, not twenty minutes after it had happened, in fact. The bank where Alissa had gone to make a withdrawal had just opened when a customer rushed in and shouted for the teller to call an ambulance—a man had just collapsed getting out of a car on the bank parking lot. The man of course was Archy Norton, and even though Alfred Cornbloom, who was driving the car, had the presence of mind to pull Archy back in, then drive straight across the street to the fire station where artificial respiration was administered by Paul Martini, it was too late. Archy was gone.

In an incredible coincidence, Archy, Alfred Cornbloom, Paul Martini, even Alissa Lipsmeier's husband Howard, were members of the local Rotary chapter, along with Bill Wilson. Is that why Peggy Wilson waits so long to tell her husband, who was working in his office at the back of the house when she received the call from Alissa?

"Archy Norton! Impossible! Ha!" he laughs and stares out the window a moment, then seems to shrug it off and returns to the sandwich he is making at the counter. He has just placed the edge of the knife on the upper left corner of the sandwich, raised his shoulder slightly in preparation for plunging the knife through the bread, when he stops.

He throws the knife down and marches over to the breakfast table where his daughter Angela, home from college for the holidays, is slowly stirring a cup of instant soup. He sits down beside her, pulls his chair closer to hers, then a bit closer yet, gently closes his hands over hers to force her to stop stirring the soup. Steam rises slowly about their joined hands as Angela looks up in surprise.

But her father isn't looking at her. He's looking across the kitchen at his wife, Peggy. He releases Angela's hand and instead grabs the back of her chair.

"Right here," he says, smiling at Peggy. "He was sitting *right here* and I was'—and now he releases Angela's chair and makes an energetic up and down motion above his lap with his parted hands, palms vertical—*"right here.* Yesterday. Twenty-four hours ago, almost to the minute. This close to one another. . ."

Obviously, Bill is speaking of the Wednesday Rotary luncheon where, quite likely, he saw Archy Norton for the last time.

Peggy nods sadly, sighs, "Yes. It must be terrible for Joanne— the day before Christmas."

Joanne is Archy Norton's wife. Indeed, it must be terrible, terrible for her, but Bill doesn't seem to be thinking about this. In fact, even though he is still looking right at Peggy with that smile on his face that is so difficult—impossible really—to describe, he hardly seems to have heard her.

" 'Would you pass me the butter, Bill,' he says, 'though I'll give you two to one it's margarine.' A joke, you see. We'd just been arguing about the new casino bill—he's big against it, of course—and. . . but arguing is too strong a word. . ."

Bill just couldn't get over it. Only twenty-four hours before, sitting no farther from him than here to here. And the strangest thing that he'd be sitting near him at all. Bill had gotten to the meeting late, and the only seat left was next to Archy. Not that they didn't get along, far from it, but Bill had his circle of friends and Archy his, and they didn't have the same interests or opinions on political issues. And that's why we could hardly desribe Archy and Bill as friends in any fundamental sense of the word. Friendly acquaintances would be more accurate—perhaps even casual acquaintances.

Which makes Bill's reaction to Archy's death so puzzling, but no more so—less, in fact—than Peggy's. Bill, after all, was sitting right next to the man just twenty-four hours before, which could surely be a bit disconcerting.

So why does Peggy wait almost three hours to give Bill the news? Alissa Lipsmeier called her with the tragic news a few minutes past nine. Peggy takes the call at the telephone in the kitchen, which is only a dozen steps from Bill's office at the back of the house, yet she waits until almost noon before finally breaking the news to him—very nearly three hours. During this time she calls two friends—Kate Frederick and Lucy O'Day—to break the news, then calls Alissa Lipsmeier back and talks the longest time—at one point she's almost in tears—but still she does not tell her husband. What's more, Bill has a phone in his office, receiving numerous calls during the day, and it was certainly quite possible—even likely—that in three hours' time someone would call with the news of Archy Norton's death. And if that happened, when he came out of the office to tell Peggy the news, as he assuredly would have, then how could she explain that she already knew but didn't tell him? He would know by her reaction—there was no way to hide it—and what would he say then?

In waiting three hours to tell Bill the news of Archy Norton's death, Peggy has quite obviously run a terrible, terrible risk.

But we can't say just why.

Nothing seems to explain her reaction to the news, her delay in telling her husband, her bleak mood the rest of the day, Bill's desiccated laughter, perplexity, and horror—yes, horror—at hearing the news of the death of a person who meant nothing, really, to either of them.

Oh, Peggy did know Archy's wife, of course, we must admit that, and it would be only natural for her to feel for and even identify with a woman suddenly bereft of husband, lover, father of her children—and on Christmas Eve!—and of course Bill had had the kidney removed less than a year before—was on his back for a month and had to take things easy for a good while after that—so it would be natural, absolutely natural, for both Bill and Peggy to think of his own recent medical problems when the news came of Archy Norton's death. But still it just simply does not add up because while we must admit the naturalness of those thoughts we must also recall that Archy Norton was not the only person to die in the almost full year since Bill's surgery—and complete recovery, just the picture of health now—and some who had died—Bill's cousin Clarence Jones, for instance, who had been like a brother to him—were much closer, had much greater claims on Bill's and Peggy's affections and fears.

And maybe it's because it just does not add up that Bill and Peggy do not mention the horrible news the rest of the day, not once, until late that night when they are both in bed, Peggy reading and Bill lying on his back with his right arm thrown over his forehead as if shielding his eyes from the sun. We cannot tell if his eyes are open, not even when he begins to speak.

"So, Archy Norton. . ." he says.

"Yes," Peggy agrees, "Archy Norton. . ."

* * *

On Christmas Day we celebrate the birth of the Son of God. On that day, surely, we can be free of thoughts of death, especially the death of Archy Norton, a casual acquaintance.

Indeed, with the traditional big Christmas breakfast of sausage links, bacon, scrambled eggs, hash browns, waffles, and coffee cake, then opening presents, followed by a furious three hours of cooking and cleaning in preparation for the annual invasion of Bill's brothers, sisters and their families from Connecticut, there is hardly time to catch one's breath, much less brood over an event that makes no reasonable or profound claim on our emotions. So we are not surprised when Christmas day passes with no further mention of Archy Norton. So too does the morning and afternoon of the next day, and we could be forgiven for supposing that the regrettable affair is over with now. But we would be wrong.

That evening of the day after Christmas the Wilsons have over for dinner their best friends, Dr. Moses Cohen and his wife Sally, along with the Cohens' daughter and son-in-law who've just flown in from California. During a lull in the conversation, without really planning to perhaps, Peggy mentions the tragic death of Archy Norton.

Sally Cohen lowers her face into the palms of her hands, and

Bill and Moses simultaneously lay their knives and forks down with an air of finality as if to say, "Now it's out in the open. Now we can dispense with this charade of normality and get to the *thing*."

They begin talking, all four of them. Sally Cohen's eyes brim with tears—and it's only then that Peggy remembers that Sally knows Joanne Norton much better than she herself does. Yet she also seems to recall that Sally doesn't like her very well; wasn't "sour" the word Sally had used for her once? Hadn't there been a meeting of the Rotary Anns at which Joanne made some disparaging remark about Sally's cold pumpkin soup? So Peggy cannot understand Sally's grief—we'll call it grief although that does not seem quite accurate—any more than we can understand the tears that well in Peggy's eyes or the obsessive, morbid *enthusiasm*—call it that—with which Bill and Moses launch into an explanation, almost compete with one another to explain to the son-in-law who Archy Norton was and what has become of him.

We pity the son-in-law, pinned in the far right corner of the dining room table, as Bill and Moses strain across the table to explain the tragic situation, which, surely, is of no interest to him since he obviously didn't know the man. Yet, despite the fact that it is obviously terribly important to them that the son-in-law understand—what? everything—we learn nothing. Nothing explains anything. Not only was Archy Norton not a close friend to either Bill or Moses, it turns out, but he was not particularly admired by either. He was something of a "bumbler," in Dr. Cohen's words, well meaning but ineffectual; in the many Rotary service projects—Moses Cohen is in fact this year's president of the Rotary chapter—it was better that Archy stay out of the way. Sally Cohen worries that Joanne Norton may have been left ill-provided for. Bill and Moses recall that Archy was always forgetting to pay his Rotary dues. Suddenly, Bill remembers Archy Norton's quixotic campaign for state representative some years before. As an independent, yet! Against beloved old Teddy Brennan, who'd held the seat for four terms and had the entire Democratic party machine behind him! Yes, now they all worry that Joanne Norton may indeed have been left ill-provided for.

Still, the Cohens must also acknowledge that Archy Norton was awfully kind to their son, Larry, who is, in fact, so upset at the news—even now, over two full days after the event—that he has not come to dinner tonight even though he was invited and eagerly awaited by Angela Wilson, who, we must remember, is also sitting at the table and listening to the endless anecdotes about Archy Norton and seems to be strangely disturbed by the talk, which is, to say the least, puzzling.

There may be a complex, almost labyrinthine chain of reasoning (associations, emotions, motives) behind Angela's otherwise baffling reaction to the talk. (We see her frequently press her temples with her fingertips as if her head is simply killing her.) Certain facts may be important. Angela Wilson and Larry Cohen were once an "item," very nearly engaged, we seem to recall. They didn't "break up" so much as "drift apart"—a phenomenon that had nothing at all to do with Larry's twice failing the state bar exam and thus having no real prospects as a head-of-household. In fact, Larry did finally pass the bar exam on the third try and set up an office in the finished basement of his parents' house, which is one reason why Angela was so anxious to see him once again, to congratulate him, wish him the best. This she cannot do, of course, because he is too upset to come, upset by the death of Archy Norton, who, it now comes out, had taken Larry under his wing so to speak, had shown him the ropes, sent a little business his way, and even "wet-nursed him'—the phrase is Sally's—through his first court appearance. But the man so admired by Larry is Archy Norton the ambulance chaser, a bumbler (and strangely enough the label used by Dr. Cohen is one that Angela's father had once applied to Larry) a well-meaning incompetent who, it's altogether likely, died without leaving his wife adequately provided for—and what kind of model for a young man such as Larry? Are we (Angela) to think that Larry is so desperate, so incompetent himself as to look up to such a man, thus implying that his own prospects are bleak, making him hardly a catch for Angela who, it is just possible we now realize, still has some lingering feelings for the Cohens' son?

When we think about it though, this tortuous explanation seems unlikely. As soon as the Cohen's walked through the door, after all, they apologized for Larry's absence, giving the reason we noted above, to which Angela responded with no more than a polite expression of disappointment. She does not seem at all affected by Larry's absence. Indeed, now that we think of it, it is not so much Sally Cohen's account of Larry's attachment to Archy that apparently has upset Angela but, rather, the talk of the death itself. Yes, now that we think of it, now that we think of it, now that we think of it, Angela's behavior was altogether strange at lunch the day before Christmas when her mother finally broke the news to Bill about Archy's death, at which point, recall, Bill sat down next to Angela and re-enacted the macrabre little scene that transpired between him and Archy Norton almost exactly twenty-four hours before at the weekly Rotary luncheon. And who, in the re-enactment, represented Archy Norton? Angela, of course. Horrible, horrible!

The only logical explanation for Angela's behavior over the last two days—for, now that we think of it, her behavior at dinner is merely a continuation of a black mood of longer standing—is that she has fallen under the same inexplicable and now obviously pervasive spell that seems to have stunned not only her parents but also Dr. and Mrs. Cohen, their son Larry, their son-in-law, who now looks positively ill, and her brother Billy, only seven years old, who should, one would think, long ago have asked to leave the table to play or watch television but has not, no indeed, has instead listened to every word of the account of the death of Archy Norton with fascination and, we are afraid, dismay.

And surely his reaction is the most puzzling of all, a young boy with no experience of death, no reason to fear his own death or even his parents'—a natural enough fear in children—even though his father had the kidney removed hardly a year ago. We have already noted that his father's recovery is total, complete, and that he is the picture of health. If we strained for some explanation of the son's exaggerated reaction to the talk of Archy Norton's death—and we must acknowledge at the outset that an explanation strained after is perforce suspect, hardly worth considering— we might note that the son is acutely aware of his parents' advanced age, in relative terms. His father is almost sixty—but the picture of health—and his mother fifty; they are often mistaken for Billy's grandparents. But this fact is surely no more than an embarrassment—and quite likely not even that—to Billy, who in fact jokes about it with his friends, sister, and even his parents.

It is indeed straining after an explanation to attribute to his father's recent health problems or his parents' age Billy's excessive distress at the talk of Archy Norton's death—distress so severe that Billy eventually is noted by his mother to be perspiring and trembling, his lips blue: a sure sign, she thinks, that he is coming down with something, the latest "bug," no doubt, at which conclusion she carts her son off to bed, ending the discussion of Archy Norton, for good, we sincerely pray.

* * *

We are not fooled by the fact that Archy Norton is not mentioned once in the Wilsons' house over the next thirty-six hours between the Saturday night dinner and his funeral on Monday morning. The joyless, anxious brooding that characterizes each of the Wilsons over this period is a dead giveaway—of something. Bill stays in his office virtually the whole time, although he can hardly be said to be working. Peggy worries from refrigerator to range to counter, making far too much food, which her family only picks at. Angela, in fact, is not seen to eat a solitary morsel—except for a single slice of American cheese—the while. Billy spends all of Sunday afternoon doing pages of simple addition from his math book, doubly puzzling since he hates math and has already done these pages, getting all the answers correct, which we could hardly guess from the way he goes over and over each one, figuring the sums on his fingers and frowning, as if he does not trust the answers.

What are we to make of all this?

We would be more perplexed and worried about the Wilson family, though, if we didn't know that the funeral of Archy Norton is quickly approaching. The funeral will be a climax and expiation of grief, surely, a painful leave-taking but also a cleansing and renewal. The Nortons will go on as go on they must, and the Wilson family will cast off the gloom, the mood—whatever it is— and return to normal. Or so we hope and pray.

Angela and Billy give us cause to doubt our hopes, though. After their parents have gone to the funeral, instead of playing or watching television or visiting friends as young people should do on holiday, they sit in virtual silence, waiting, obviously, for their parents' return.

A little before noon they hear their parents' car pull into the drive. Angela goes to open the front door for them. "How was the funeral?" she asks, then blushes at the absurdity of the question. "I know, I know," her mother says. *What* does she know?

Bill walks through the family room and into the living room where, unaccountably (because it is used only for guests), Billy is now sitting on the far corner of the sofa. Bill walks past him and stares out the window.

"It was a beautiful ceremony, I thought," he begins. He seems to be talking to the window but evidently is speaking to Billy, who turns his head and raises his face toward his father without surprise, as if this is truly what he has been waiting for. "Each of his sons said a little—what would you call it? not a speech really— about him. An anecdote, a little story, you know? I thought they did a real nice job. Oh, the youngest one broke down a little bit, but that's to be expected. The youngest went first, then the next one, then the oldest. The youngest one told about the time. . ."

Bill seems to remember every single word of the Norton sons' eulogies. It takes him a good while to get through the first son's eulogy, and even longer on the second because the more Bill talks the more he embellishes—the stiffling heat in the church, the abundance, variety, and color of the flowers, some of his own memories of Archy, and on and on.

Billy doesn't seem to mind, though. He sits quietly and listens to every word. Still, we cannot be absolutely sure that his father's words are meant for him alone. Bill is talking to the window, after all, and what's more before he's finished reciting the youngest son's eulogy Peggy has appeared in the door of the living room and, instead of passing on by on her way to the kitchen where she should begin preparing lunch, she stops to listen. At the point that Bill begins describing the gigantic spray of chrysanthemums sent by the Rotary, Peggy has edged into the living room, Angela has taken her place in the doorway, and, yes, now we can clearly detect behind Angela the Cohens—Moses, Sally, and Larry—who must have returned from the funeral with Bill and Peggy. Billy strains toward his father, Peggy edges forward, Angela edges forward, the Cohens edge forward, we edge forward. We all gather round and listen, knowing that we are likely to understand nothing but that we can't help ourselves, the thing has happened, we have suffered a blow, somehow, by this death of a casual acquaintance on the day before Christmas, we have been damaged by it, and we will never never recover.

A FIN DE SIECLE ZODIAC

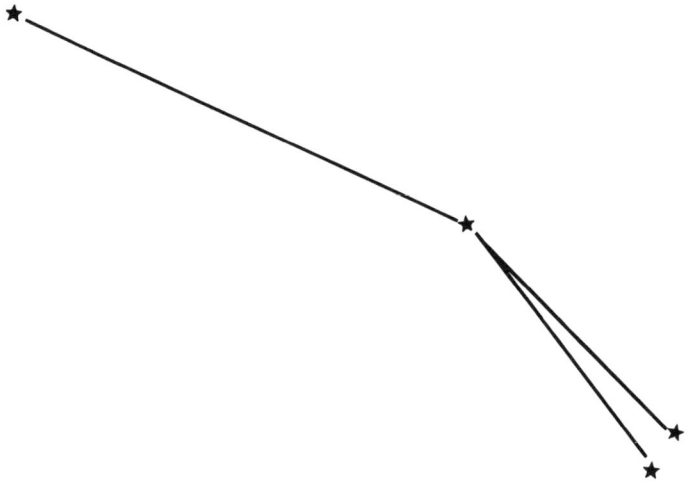

I.
The Water Witch
(March 21-April 20)

He found himself still alive, long past the time when anyone believed in him.

Years past, in an age of faith, Oklahoma farmers paid his grandfather to cross their dusty fields--him in his bib overalls skipping along barefoot after the old man—and mark with trembling wand the most unlikely spot—beneath a scattering of flint, in the shade of a stunted Rose-of-Sharon, between two graves, unmarked, left from the Indian wars—where only the true believer would bother to dig. And, when he was young, the faithful always found water.

But Johnny barely remembers Oklahoma.

"Crazy old bastard," his father said in 1922, turning his back on the old man and a way of life that he could no longer bear and taking his wife, daughter and young son to Kansas City, where he found work in an ice plant. Johnny's mother ran off that summer with an itinerant preacher. He remembers her less well than the smell of the black leather Bible, pungent with sweat, that the preacher left behind as if in exchange for the woman he took with him.

Johnny kept the Bible for many years, although he never opened it. He would press it to his face and remember his mother and, more vividly, the tent revival his grandfather took him to in Oklahoma where a man in a black suit would raise the holy book like a hatchet over his head and chase the devil out into the cicada-thundering night.

He lost his one chance at love because in a moment of pure, purblind honesty he told his beloved that more than all the world he wanted to be a water witch. He lived alone throughout the Second World War, exempted from service because of his work in a defense plant, almost bitter at lost love but not quite because he knew that more glorious than love is the sound of water gurgling up through dry stone.

In the hot, dry summer of 1946 he left Kansas City and worked his way south, using, instead of the forked hickory branch favored by his grandfather, a metal pants press for a wand. He did a little business. Outside Butler, Missouri, a farmer charged his neighbors twenty-five cents a head to watch him do his magic. He thought he had acquired a following until he realized that they had paid to gawk at the *Kansas City Star* reporter who came down to do a piece on "crazy John Starling the water witch." They crowded round, hoping to get in the picture, as the reporter snapped him in rage and dispair twisting the pants press into a tangle of steel ribbon.

He cannot believe that almost a half a century has passed since then. Now, no one has faith in him, in his magic, except, of course, for three men in Texas, one in Utah, a commune in Oregon, a family living in a cave in the Arkansas Ozarks, and an oil billionaire from the Mid-East. He is skeptical of all but the latter, who cables him that his services are required to restore his desert kingdom to the green garden of myth and song. A cashier's check is being forwarded, the cablegram says.

* * *

If you are born under the sign of the Water Witch—a water sign, of course—you have an affinity for not only water but also ice, the odor of sweat, the thunder of cicadas, and, curiously enough, dust, whose lure you can hardly resist. You are sometimes stunned to think that you have centered your life on a bright but indistinct memory of an age that was dying as you were born. Every day you check your mailbox, waiting patiently, without hope, for the check from the one true believer in a distant land.

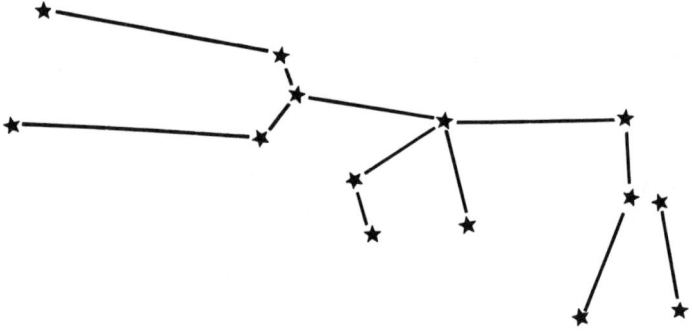

II.
The Low-Rider (with Fog Lights)
(April 21-May 21)

A spring sign, the Low-Rider (with Fog Lights) is best seen on warm, cloudless nights in the barrio, East L. A.

We say "barrio" quite easily, with a sort of smug grin, as if we are as familiar with the place as we are with the word, which we would like to give a certain twist to, lower our voice and let it resonate nasally as when we say "sangfroid"—but we are not sure if one does that with Spanish. The fact is, we are not really comfortable with the word "barrio" and even less comfortable with the place, to which we have never been.

We are not at all comfortable with the low-riders. We are not even sure if that is the proper term. "Low-rider." Is that it?

If we are not mistaken the low-rider is vaguely related—*similar,* not really *related* at all—to what we called a "jalopy" in a happier time. The word itself—"jalopy"—makes us smile contentedly and nostalgically as our thoughts turn to malt shops, sock-hops, letterman's sweaters, Archie, Jughead, Betty, and Veronica. Our heros then were Kyle Rote, Doak Walker, Billy Vessels, Mickey Mantle, Bob Cousy, and Bob Pettit.

These low-riders, though. (Is that what they are called?) They are low in the front, we seem to remember, but doesn't the rear rise up absurdly high? The high rear/low front design gives the impression that they are capable of running up under something and turning it over, like a huge, mobile lever or malicious, powerful scoop. And what about those fog lights, which seem to have no legitimate function, which serve only to probe at us, pry into places where the low-rider does not really belong, finally, perhaps, to blind us?

Didn't we read (or see it on *Sixty Minutes,* perhaps) that many of the low-riders are equiped with a certain apparatus that allows them to bounce up and down as they prowl slowly down the street, or even more absurdly, to bounce in place? What purpose does this bouncing serve? It seems to be a conscious affront to something. At the very least it gives the impression of hostility, of aggression about to be unleashed, as if the low-rider is gathering itself for a charge, to blind us, flip us over.

[Strike that last, a fatuous comment.]

We should make it clear that we wish the low-rider well. That, in fact, is why the bouncing disturbs us. The apparatus that allows the bouncing must be quite expensive, and we do not think this expense is totally justified. Surely the barrio can find better uses for its money. Its needs, we understand, are great. It does not have enough of. . . it lacks sufficient. . .Well, quite obviously the needs of the barrio are great.

At least we *think* that such is the case. We have not been to East L. A., of course. And we have no plans to go there. It is out of our way. We live far from East L. A. In fact, we are moving soon, by coincidence farther still.

* * *

If you are born under the sign of the Low-Rider (with Fog Lights)—a fire sign, volatile and destructive—you are probably brown, black, yellow, or red. This is not your fault and we do not hold it against you. We wish you the best, but we have to be honest:

There are countries where you would fit in better than here, where you are more likely to prosper and be happy. In retrospect, your coming here was probably a mistake.

III.
AIDS
(May 22-June 21)

. . .yes, my brethren, I know it's hot, and getting close to noon, and you can just taste that fried chicken or that roast and gravy, that apple pie. . .

> [*Tittering and good-natured smiles exchanged among the congregation.*]

. . .but while we're talking about how the world has changed since I was a boy, I've got one last thing on my mind, something I've got to get off my chest. Old as I am, and I know you young folks making all that noise up in the balcony think I'm *awful* old and cranky. . .

> [*From the floor of the auditorium heads crane back and up, fire angry looks into the balcony, and the horseplay suddenly stops.*]

. . .but old as I am there's still a thing or two I just don't understand. Let me tell you what I saw in to Columbus just the other day. Yessir, right there in broad daylight on the streets of our own Columbus, Mississippi, was two men walking down the street holding hands. Holding hands! You know what that means—I don't have to spell it out for you. Got young boys and girls here with us today who don't need to be hearing about that sort of behavior, supposing they could hear it for all the racket they're making up in the balcony. But praise Jesus, somebody please tell me what's happening in the world. In broad daylight, I tell you! I'm not a cruel man, my brothers and sisters, I'm not a merciless man. I love those two men that I saw holding hands like I love the least of these, as Lord God commands us to. I'm not a cruel man, but I say unto you this: We all ought to get down on our knees right here today and thank God for sending us AIDS. . .

[*Immediately, several in the congregation stumble out into the aisles and kneel down. "Amen!" "Praise God, praise him!"*]

. . . for sending us AIDS as a bright shining light to show us the way, to guide these lost sheep back to the true path of righteousness for His name's sake oh Lord! I tell you, my friends, I just don't understand it. With all the bounteous beauties of God's great glorious creation—and nothing more beautiful to a man than a woman or to a woman than a man—how can a person turn to his own sex for love and companionship? I don't, I can't, I won't understand it! They can't help themselves, they say. "I cain't help myself! I cain't help myself!"

[*Here he screws up his face like a child and minces his way around the pulpit. Laughter from the congregation.*]

Now I tell you, that'll work just fine for a couple of years, but by the time you hit three or four, that don't cut it no more. I couldn't help this withered arm I was born with, and I shed a few tears over it, let me tell you, but that didn't change a blessed thing. I went on. Sometimes you gotta get past "I cain't help it" and just go on. "I was different when I was young," they say. Horsefeathers. Let *me* tell you about different. Try a boy with a withered arm that kneels down in the middle of school to pray to Jesus for different. I was called every name in the book. Made me eat grass, made me eat dirt. Smeared dog stuff in my hair. Slap my face over and over until I'd cry. Sit on my belly so I couldn't breathe, till I'd pass out. That was recess for me, day after day, year in, year out. Different, huh! Say, "I was lonely, didn't have nobody." If being lonely'll turn you into a homosexual, there's a lot of us in a hell of a lot of trouble. I was lonely every day of my life until I was twenty-six. Married the sweetest little girl that ever drew breath. She was with child right away. George we were going to call him if he was a boy, Lois if it was a girl. Can't hear those names today without wanting to cry, my heart aches so. She died, you know, got a hemorrhage and bled to death, baby gone with her, while I was off ministering to a drunkard that'd burned down his barn. I can't smell whiskey on someone's breath today without thinking of my sweet Doris, the only light of my life, and the names I never got to sing over a sleeping child: George and Lois, George and Lois, George and Lois. So...You're different, you're lonely, is that it? They'll tell it like it's some brand spanking new story that nobody's ever heard before, ever whispered over the meatloaf you cooked yourself and ate yourself alone, the hundredth meal in a row you ate alone, "I couldn't help myself, I was different, I was lonely, then out of the grey, dreary sad world there stepped one person who'd take my hand and walk with me on down the road a ways, one brief bright moment of love before the dark closes in again..."

[*Suddenly, he weeps.*]

* * *

AIDS is, of course, an earth sign. Dust to dust. Let us pray.

IV.
The Career Woman (in Skirt)
(June 22-July 22)

She is best seen rising in the southern sky, due east of Canis
Minor, at 9:30 p.m., December 30th. Probably she has just left the
office New Year's Eve party (held just down the street, actually,
at the tony Duke's Grill, and of course on the 30th this year, a Friday, since no one will be working on Saturday, except perhaps Jane
Duffy-Carson, the career woman, who feels guilt—or make that
fear—when she does not work on Saturdays.

She had arisen early that day to make sure that everything was
in order, all neatly packed in the collapsible travel bag—the black
lingerie and hose to go with the black tuxedo ensemble of jacket
with ruffled lace bustle, black-satin tapered slacks pegged at the
ankle, black pumps with the two-and-one-half-inch heels, and the
white silk blouse with the tiny bow tie. She had removed everything from the bag and carefully hung the clothes in her office
closet, intending to change just before the party, where she would

be a *sensation.*

But at the last moment she becomes frightened. She stares at herself in the full-length mirror that hangs on the inside of her office door: naked, the brown halos of her nipples, the dark wedge of pubic hair. She puts on the black panties, then, braless, the white silk blouse and bow tie. Then the jacket. The slight draft from the ceiling vent wafts the ridiculous bustle against the back of her bare legs.

She knows that she will never wear the satin slacks, pegged at the ankle, although she adores them. Her associates have never seen her in slacks of any kind, not even at the summer picnic for mid-level executives held at the board chairman's estate; while everyone else gamboled about in blue jeans, designer overalls, even cutoffs, she wore a sun dress, got poison ivy on her legs, and for the next blistering-hot two weeks was driven mad by her panty hose.

Jane has always dressed for success. She favors wool suits and wool-blend blazers and skirts in the winter, linen suits in summer, occasionally a severely tailored dress and short jacket, at the most casual a skirt, silk-blend blouse, and cardigan sweater. The one essential is the skirt, which she hates above all things of this world.

She knows what the skirt is for: easy access by the groping hand, the prying eye.

She became aware of the role of the skirt in junior high school, where there was a great deal of talk about "shooting beaver." Who shot beaver, of whom and how, when, why, and with what result. There seemed to be a whole arcana of beaver shooting that left her confused and vaguely humiliated and angered. The jokes— "You've got to eat any beaver you shoot'; "Any beaver you shoot you have to take home and mount over the mantle"—made her physically ill.

Even by the late Sixties her high school forbade the wearing of slacks by girls. When Jane's good friend Shelly Ward wore slacks one day, she was sent home to change. She returned that afternoon in a full-skirted dress with no panties underneath and sat through Mr. Arnold's geometry class showing everything to everybody. "That's really the point, isn't it?" she said to the principal, Mr. Jameson, right before he suspended her for three days. When she came back, the other girls would have nothing to do with her. Jane steered clear of her too.

Jane knows all the rules to everything, and this has allowed her to climb the corporate ladder quickly.

She thinks of herself as a feminist but becomes disturbed, even depressed, at the idea of being thought a feminist—but she does not know why.

She says nothing when Steve Perini puts his hand on the inside of her thigh, under the table, at the Wednesday morning conference. Although she is outraged, she is too puzzled to act. Steve is neither below nor above her on the corporate ladder, and they do not even work in the same department, so this cannot be some career strategy. She thinks it might be a sex thing. But she's not sure.

Jane has not married, although she thinks she might like to one day. ('Duffy" of Jane Duffy-Carson is her mother's maiden name, which Jane appended to her own after getting her M.B.A; she has never gotten along with her mother, however.) She thinks that she ought not miss the experience of giving birth, although she is uncomfortable around children and she knows that she could never put her heels up in those stirrup things. (She dreamt once of asking the doctor if it would be all right for her to wear an ankle-length, pleated skirt for the delivery.)

She thinks somehow that everything in the world is related to skirts, but nothing is related to her.

She leaves the New Year's Eve party early, at 9:30. It occurs to her as she walks down the street toward her BMW, holding her skirt against the bitter wind, that she always leaves the party early.

* * *

If you are born under the sign of the Career Woman (in Skirt), an air sign, you will fear strong winds. You will yearn for one bright, hard memory, one moment of intense feeling, to anchor you here among the living, to keep you from being blown up, up high and away from all you never desired, all you never suffered.

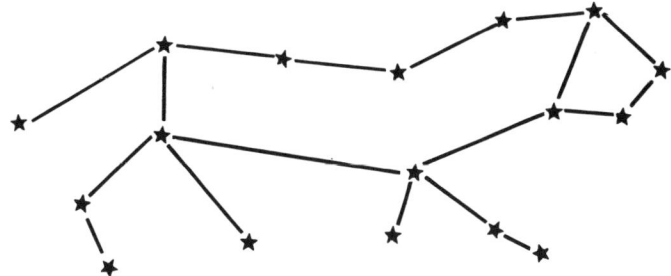

V.
Pit Bull
(July 23-August 23)

Yeh, I own one or two. And now you're going to tell me that you're passing an ordinance against them, right? Fine with me. Hey, if it makes you happy, who am I to complain?

Let me tell you a few more things it doesn't make a fuckin' A to me whether you pass a law against it. Cigarettes. I'm going to smoke my cigarettes in my home, in my car, at the supermarket, in the restaurant, *any time, any place I want to.* Did you get that? If not, then go back and read it again. Guns. We really don't have to go over this again, do we? You want to get cozy with Castro? Fine. You want to watch Nicaragua parade through Dallas, Texas? Fine. The parade stops at my front door though, wimpo. You want some hop-head breaking into your home and raping your wife? Yeh, you probably would. You'd probably get off on that. Probably the only way you could get it up.

Pay attention, now, and you might learn something. (It won't take long. You're too boring to talk to very long.) There are two types of people: those that'll fight for their freedoms (me) and those that'll fight to take them away (you). Check that. You won't *fight* for anything. You just finagle, and haggle, and whine, and chip chip chip away at whatever's bigger and stronger than you, shovel words and more words until a good man just about gives up, like *you* do, you've given up on everything already, you're afraid of everything—my guns, my dogs, my cigarettes—so you'll pass a law against all of them, and pass one to make me wear a seat belt (which I ain't gonna do), and pass one to make me wear a motor-cyle helmet (which I ain't gonna do), and pass a law against every breath a free man takes while you're lined up out in the rain with a candle in your hand shedding a tear (boo hoo!) for poor Willi Washington Lincoln Jackson who got the chair for raping and murdering twenty or thirty people. Sure, but when the *real* shooting comes along you'll want me in the front lines crawling on my belly then, and you know what?—I'll be happy to oblige—and you know why?—because I *like* to kill those runty slant-eyed dinks because every time I get one in the V of my sights I think of your face, and I squeeze that trigger just as lovingly as you sucked your mama's titty when you were ten years old.

What's that? You say my pit bull just bit your little Percival who was running across my lawn? Oooh, sooo sorry!

* * *

The Pit Bull is a water sign, because my dog takes a piss wherever it damn well pleases. If you're born under this sign, congratulations, just stay the fuck out of my way.

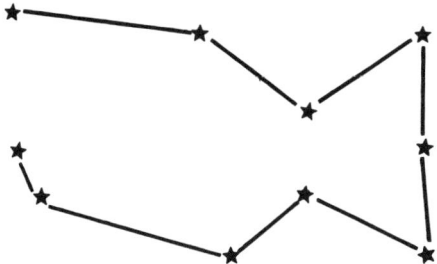

VI.
Marilyn Monroe
(August 24-September 23)

   Although her dream was not yet realized, she had already made it farther than anyone would have predicted: all the way to Houck, Arizona, just a few miles over the border from Gallup, New Mexico. It wasn't Hollywood, wasn't even California, but no one could deny that Dawn had come a long way on $38, a thumb, and more guts, spunk, and pretty than anybody would expect in a seventeen-year-old high school drop-out from Rolla, Missouri.

   Actually, she'd run out of money before she hit New Mexico, but that'd been no problem. With a world full of friendly truckers, she could have gone across the U. S. and back on a song and a smile. One, two more rides would have taken her to California, easy, but the "Help Wanted" sign at the convenience store just outside of Houck had caught her eye.

   On-the-Way was the name of the store. It was really a Git-n-Go which had gone under, been bought up by Charlie Sellers, and expanded by the addition of a grill, counter, and four stools. Charlie manned the cash register while Dawn worked behind the counter, although each would take over the whole operation if the other was gone for any reason. "The second you walk out the door there's twenty girls waiting for this job," he'd tell her as he led her into the storeroom or out to his Bronco for a "quickie," as he did two or three times a week. She'd weep piteously afterward, modeling her performance first on Faye Dunaway in *Chinatown,* then on Meryl Streep in *The French Lieutenant's Woman,* Ingrid Bergman in *Casablanca,* and so on.

It was all good experience for her—a "well-spring of pain," she called it, which she could draw upon for her later roles—and something she would have missed out on if she'd gone straight on to California and broken into the movie business right away.

"Marilyn Monroe was raped by her father, you know," she observed, although the customer—Sonny, she was pretty sure his name was—seemed to be only half listening.

"Raped, huh?" he said, grimacing at the coffee, which Dawn knew must be terrible because everybody complained about it. Dawn didn't use caffeine, tobacco, or alcohol, although someday she planned to take some dope. She thought the experience would be good for her.

"Yes, raped. It scarred her for life. That's why she'd go from one man to another, looking for a little kindness, a little love. She was married to Joe DiMaggio and Arthur Miller, and she had sex with Clark Gable and Bobby Kennedy. I figure she wanted to try out the best man in each of the major occupations to see if she could find somebody deserving of her. Well, she never did."

Sonny swallowed a huge bite of chili dog.

"I hear Clark Gable had B. O."

"Huh!" Dawn snorted. "You should get downwind of Charlie Sellers sometime."

Dawn talked to everyone who came in. She would tell them anything about herself, even about going out to Charlie's Bronco. Sometimes she'd tell the story funny, sometimes sad, sometimes seething with fury, depending on what facet of her acting technique she was working on. Sometimes, if Charlie was out, she'd take a customer into the storeroom with her. Once she took two Indians from Gallup with her, even though Indians frightened her.

That was the reason she'd done it—the fear experience, which would be valuable to her later and might become part of her legend.

At some point before Sonny finished his Suzie Q, Dawn hiked her skirt up and began to massage her thigh, complaining that she had a cramp from standing all day.

Then they were back in the storeroom, Dawn sitting on a stack of motor oil cases, her legs wrapped around Sonny.

"Sonny, after I become famous, you can tell people that you fucked me, if you want to."

"Hunh," he grunted noncommittally.

After he finished they went back out front, and Sonny paid up. Dawn seemed more somber now—thoughtful or wistful or nostalgic.

"Sonny," she called to him as he was heading out the door. He looked back without turning around. "Ten years from now, will you come out to Hollywood to put a red rose on my grave?"

"Baby," he said, "I'll put a dozen a day on there."

She smiled happily.

* * *

If you are born under the sign of Marilyn Monroe, a fire sign, one day your name will blaze brightly for from fifteen to thirty seconds. For most of you, that will be enough.

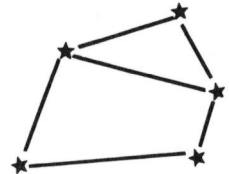

VII.
Collapsing Infrastructure
(September 24-October 23)

"Do you know that parts of the Appian Way are still used by the public? The Romans built their roads to last forever."

She obviously means this as an accusation of sorts. Her eyes snap in anger but also fear, and she hugs her clipboard to her bosom, a breastplate against attack.

But the young man—our tour guide—has apparently not taken umbrage at the lady's remarks. In fact, he slaps his head in self-deprecatory amazement and delight.

"Two thousand, twenty-five hundred years! Can you believe it? And we feel lucky to get a few decades out of"—and here he waves the hubcap-sized flake of rust that he'd pulled from one of the foundation supports of the Williamsburg Bridge at the beginning of his lecture—"these things."

He sails the hunk of rust like a Frisbee toward the water, but a second after leaving his hand it suddenly disintegrates in a blood-red shower of dust.

We shake our heads and duly note the phenomenon on our clipboards.

"What exactly causes that?" one of us asks.

"No one knows for sure, but here's some information on it," he says, digging a pamphlet out of his briefcase. "Anyone else like one?"

We all take one and clip it under the other pamphlets and handouts we'd collected at earlier stops on the tour.

"Well, now at least you know why I take the subway instead of driving in to work!" the man who'd asked the previous question jokes.

We all laugh, but our guide wags a finger knowingly.

"Ah, the subway! Our next stop."

We follow him down into the subway. It is familiarly dark and dank. Ancient, rickety subway trains lurch in and out, pasted together with graffiti. Even when the trains are gone, there is a general, profound rattle and cough in the air as if the veinous system were sick with some inexplicable but probably fatal virus.

"Four billion dollars," our guide says. "Four billion within five years, or you won't take the subway in to work either. And that's just for the most basic repairs to the trains and track. The tunnels themselves—well, enough said."

We all know that he's referring to the cave-in that occurred only a couple of miles from here on Flatbush last year. In concert, we shudder, shake our heads, then follow him up out of the subway and then down into an enormous underground complex in the Bronx where gigantic humpbacked machines—water pumps we are told—throb away row on row into the distance. All the water serving New York City comes into this pump station, fed by two huge pipes each taller than a man, then is directed out to the various sections of the city.

"The two feeder pipes leak an estimated six million gallons of water a day, all the seventeen pumps need repair, and at least half need replacing immediately," our tour guide says proudly. "Seven billion just to keep us at the present rate of deterioration."

We jot this information down on our clipboards.

"How long can the present system last without a major disaster?" I ask, only my third question of the tour.

"No one knows!" the guide says, but gives me (all of us) a handout comprising 30-40 sheets of paper held together with a huge spring clip. Then he throws his hands up at his forgetfulness and gives each of us two handouts on the ruinous subway system.

We follow him on down to the Empire State Building. He slaps its flank fondly and invites us to gaze up along the edge of the building, which we now see is visibly leaning to the east.

"How long before she goes?"

"No one knows," he says, reaching for pamphlets; but, suddenly, we all realize what has happened.

"A rhyme!"

The grey mood that had been deepening over the course of the tour (now almost half completed) breaks into splinters of bright laughter as we link arms and—the support cables singing in the air as they snap over our heads—advance two by two across the Verazzano Narrows Bridge, flinging a leaf-storm of pamphlets and handouts out over the waters and raising our voices in verse after verse of our new anthem:

> How long before she goes?
> No one knows!
>
> How long before she goes?
> No one knows!
>
> [etc.]

* * *

If you are born under the sign of Collapsing Infrastructure—an earth sign (rust, dust, broken stone)—you should seek employment in the information economy. Your fear of carpenters, mechanics, and plumbers is offset by your remarkable ability to ignore the catastrophe looming over you, under you.

VIII.
Not-Death
(October 24-November 22)

Even the grandly inventive ancients could not keep up the pretense. After spinning such absurdities as "water sign" (scorpions love to frolic in the water, of course), and adding paradox to absurdity (a *fixed* water sign), then trying to soften the blow by telling those of us born in the eighth house that we'd be marvelous company at parties, excellent doctors and cooks, they'd finally get around to the truth. Scorpio, as Barbault put it, is "the cemetery of the Zodiac." It is the House of Death.

Our century will not tolerate talk of death, though. We hide away our dying as if they have somehow failed us, as if their dying is a sort of regrettable *faux pas* or—let's admit it—somehow obscene.

Therefore, in the spirit of the age, let's consider a new symbol for the eighth house, something lovely, grand, or if not grand then witty, something at least not distressing, not obscene: something that is not death.

But the thing has a curious shape, writhing on the rim of the southern horizon, slightly to our left, at 11:30 p.m., May Day, with a sort of tail hooked through the branches of the Bergy's apple tree (from where I sit), and then rising in a sinuous compound curve toward the Collapsing Infrastructure, where it throws up two appendages to ward off the avalanche of crumbling brick, mortar, burst stone and rust.

A curious thing but not, after all, inelegant; it has a certain grace. In fact, one could almost imagine it swaying to the celestial music, even dancing. Carmen Miranda, snapping her castanets, or Isadora Duncan. Isadora! Surely a symbol for an age such as ours, an age that has freed itself from the rigid and senseless constraints of the past. With what passion we have flung ourselves across the heavens, with what valor, heedless of everything, we raise our arms in utter abandon, not seeing the long scarf of stars dangling down from Ophiuchus, snug about our neck at one end, caught in the wheel of the racing roadster at the other, destroying ourselves utterly in our blind joyful acceleration.

So it cannot be Isadora, whose death we remember more vividly than her dance. Indeed, we would do well to avoid the living entirely—they always die. We should take our icon from the immortal, in light of which resolution we must confess that we have looked at the pattern wrong. It is not a dancer. Turn it more on its side (June 30th, 9:30 p.m., due south), it is now quite obviously a hook, with what had seemed to be raised arms really a sort of guard to cover the stump of Captain Hook's right wrist as he battles Peter Pan, forever, floating in a Disney-blue lagoon beside a Disney-green island (second to the right and straight on till morning), his "birthday present" having fizzled, Wendy plucked from the plank, the boys huzzahing for Peter with his little knife as he duels Captain Hook, forever, backs him up and in a brilliant pirouette jabs him (quite comically) in the derriere, and Captain Hook falls into the water. Tick tock.

Tick tock? Nothing, the clock reminds us, is forever. Just because we last see him splashing his way sunsetward, the clockodile in pursuit (Serpens to the ancients, coiling its way through Ophiuchus), we think it will always be so. An evasion of the G-rated Disney boys, who stop the cameras an instant before Captain Hook is caught just east of the Lesser Antilles, the mighty jaws snapping down on his scrotum and anus, the beef jerky and water bisquit sucked from his small intestine, his spine munched in dreamy leisure, his head swallowed whole, rolling into the Serpens-gut where it eyeballs the tireless clock, forever dead, tick tock.

And Wendy, Michael, Jonathan and the boys? Jonathan died of leukemia almost two years to the day from his great adventure in Neverland; Michael died at the Battle of the Somme, July 1, 1916; Wendy was run over in London in 1936 by an American tourist who "just couldn't get the hang of driving on the wrong side of the road"; after a disastrous, unconsummated marriage to a Belgian aviatrix, Peter emigrated to Rhodesia where he opened a dry-goods store and died in 1951 of a mysterious illness whose symptoms, in retrospect, closely resemble AIDS, and we are now truly desperate for a new symbol for the eighth house, desperate and pessimistic, having rejected the pattern of wrinkles on the otherwise unblemished forehead of Sandro Drebrouznian of Georgia, USSR, who was the world's oldest man until his death last Tuesday, the crack in the dressing-room mirror of Stella Havens (the Perth Songbird) whose voice was so divine and thighs so creamy that she could almost resurrect men from the grave but could not keep them from dying, "The Garden of Forking Paths" of Jorge Borges, where the path does not turn, where it does not bifurcate, where there is no time but this time, irreversible and ironclad, marching inexorably to its catastrophe of murder, death, and infinite remorse, which we suffer for having begun this whole absurd effort to find a new symbol for what does not exist, leaving us to conclude that nothing will be our sign, for, ultimately, there is nothing that is not death.

* * *

Since it does not exist, this sign is neither an air, earth, fire, nor water sign. You could not, of course, have been born under this sign, which does not exist. If you were not born under this sign, you will be a remarkable liar, and, make no mistake: the lies will help. They will not be enough, but they will help.

IX.
The Slanted Man (with Flag)
(November 23-December 21)

"Look, son, I don't want to be rude, but you're just wasting your time," Harold said.

"I got all kinds of time, Pop, you let me worry about time," the young man said.

One of the nineteen or twenty things that irritated Harold about the young man was his calling him "Pop," even though Harold's name was right there on the sign above the door as you entered, in twenty-four-inch-high red, white and blue letters for any fool to see: HAROLD'S FOREIGN CAR REPAIR.

"Just give me ten minutes of your time, Pop, and I guarantee I can show you how SunDial Systems can provide you with at least twenty percent better telephone capabilities while saving you at least twenty percent over your present telephone bills."

"No sir, I'll just stick with Ma Bell."

"You didn't hear me, Pop. I *guarantee* you at least twenty percent savings while *increasing* your telephone capabilities. I'll put it in writing."

"I don't care."

"You don't care?"

"No. Ma Bell and me go back a long way. I started with Ma Bell and I'll end up with Ma Bell."

"But what do you owe Ma Bell?"

"Not a dime. I never missed a payment."

"I don't get it."

"I know you don't, son, and that's sad. There's just so gol-derned many things that young folks your age don't understand."

"Give me a for instance."

"For instance, what it is to be an American."

The young man threw his hands up and laughed bitterly, as if this was what he had been expecting all along.

"So that's it. I might have known. You're not going to go with SunDial Systems—not even going to give me a chance—because you figure it's Japanese, even though they'll save you money and maybe allow you to keep your penny-ante business going another year or two. Ma Bell now, she's hot dogs and apple pie, right? You probably think Ma Bell's some little old lady with grey hair that lives in Peoria. Hell, Ma Bell's international, just like all of them. But I won't try to confuse you with facts, no sir. Hell, I see dinosaurs like you about twice a day. You think everything is simple, that everything just goes one way. It's like you don't stand up straight but you're sort of slanted, like you're leaning into something that isn't there and any minute somebody's going to come along and tap you on the shoulder and you'll fall over because you ain't got anything to support you, there's nothing to you, you don't know what world you're living in, you're living in the past which ain't here any more if it was ever here in the first place and...aw hell, what's the use!"

Red faced and trembling in anger, the young man turned and stormed out of the office, slamming the door after him.

Harold was speechless, stunned by the outburst, so totally unexpected. Here Harold had been on the verge of launching into a lecture himself—it was going to be something about patriotism and loyalty, something about the 48-star flag that Harold had carried back with him from Okinawa and displayed on the wall behind his desk—but the young man had beaten him to it and really laid into him. And such anger! Harold felt wronged by the young man's anger, wronged and somehow foolish because he hadn't defended himself, hadn't said a word, and there was so much to say about America and the 48-star flag that had never looked quite right to Harold since they added the extra two, looked phoney somehow, he couldn't get used to it.

Suddenly, Harold turned and reached up and ripped the flag down from the wall and ran out the door into the parking lot, then stopped. The young man's 1988 Plymouth Horizon (marketed by one of the Big Three auto makers but manufactured, of course, in Japan) was gone.

Then he saw it, a block away, roaring through the yellow light at the intersection, heading west, right into a blinding sun. Harold raised the flag to shield his eyes.

*　*　*

If you are born under this sign, an air sign (flag waving in air), you are not quite sure how things have come to such a state. You're not at all sure what state it is, but you know you don't like it. You're prepared to fight to the end, but you're suddenly afraid that the end has already come. Yesterday, or perhaps the day before.

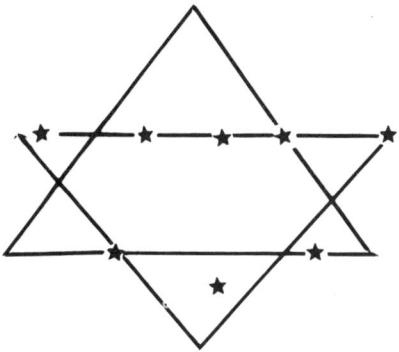

X.
The Honorary Jew
(December 22-January 20)

No one could accuse you of not having a sense of humor, and at first you took it as a sophomoric but good-natured joke. Perhaps you even started it. Wasn't it you who (borrowing from your Yeats seminar notes, no doubt) hailed Ben Ferguson on St. Pat's Day as "Oh mighty Fergus, king of the proud Red Branch kings"? To which Ferguson, never slow on the draw, replied, "Green. That's a kike name, isn't it?"

Somehow the joke became a tradition between you two. Once every week or so, in the faculty lounge most likely, he would pause, look you over appraisingly, and say, "Green. Now isn't that a kike name?"

You hadn't realized it bothered you until one day you found yourself saying, "No, it's English, Ben. Green—the color. Like Black, Brown, or White. All good English names."

Halfway through, you felt yourself blushing as, at the same

instant, Ferguson began to grin and shake his head. Then he explained to you that *Green* was actually an Anglicization of the Yiddish *Gruene* (borrowed from the German), as in *Gruenewald, Grueneblatt, Greunebaum.*

"You know, Greenwood, Greenleaf, Greentree, and, of course, Green. You mean to tell me that you didn't know that your name was Jewish?"

You compound your previous error (defending yourself when you should have ignored the boor) by now remaining silent, trying to smile and shrug but managing only a pained grimace and a spastic hunching of the shoulders.

You begin to avoid Ferguson at work, take the back stairs instead of the elevator, use the men's room on the second floor, which tends to be monopolized by students. You find yourself examining your features in the mirror over the washbasin and are cheered to be able to declare that your hair is straight and sandy-brown, your eyes hazel, and your nose rather upturned and broad. Not a bit hooked.

Still, you also recall that Cal MacNeice's wife, Sylvia, who admits to being Jewish, has blonde hair and blue eyes.

You begin to change your habits in small ways. Twice in one week you sit at the same table in the cafeteria with Mike Jacobs, whom you have never much liked, not because he is Jewish but because he has always struck you as intense, humorless, and intellectually arrogant. Now you find him to be sensitive and percipient, and you learn to appreciate his melancholy wit.

You go to the library to find self-help books on plumbing repair but come home with novels by Aharon Applefeld and Amos Oz.

You begin to listen closely to the news from the Mid-East, which disturbs you.

The next time Ferguson jokes about your name you stare at him icily. His smirk widens for a moment but then wavers, fades as he retreats in confusion. You feel you have won a small victory.

You drive six hours to Oklahoma to join marchers picketing a rally by a white supremacist group.

The next week at a cocktail party, you tell Nancy Rosen, a guest lecturer from New York, that you are Jewish.

"Liar!" she shouts and slaps you across the face.

You run to the bathroom, all your colleagues, friends, and

acquaintances staring after you, and lock yourself in. Your hands tremble, your breath is short, your chest aches. You're afraid that you might have ruined your life.

You stare at yourself in the mirror. Your eyes, you notice, are heavy with sadness and wisdom.

*   *   *

This sign, a fire sign, was ascending at the moment of our birth. We have all been made honorary Jews, a fact that we would like to forget. And, in fact, it is becoming easier for us to forget. Somewhere—over there or, closer to us, here—a man, taking comfort in our forgetfulness, is beginning to stoke up the ovens once more. Let's pretend it isn't so.

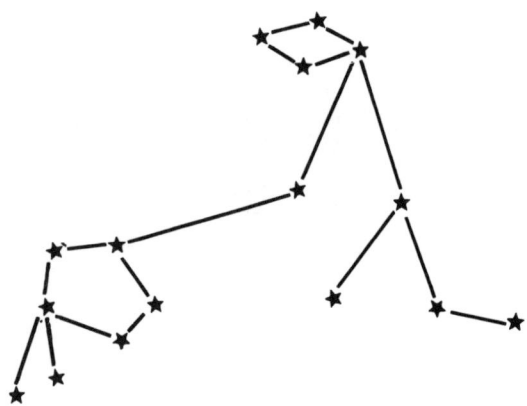

XI.
Aquarius
(January 21-February 19)

Because *something* from the past must survive,
because we do not despise it all,
because if we must build our future on the bones of the past,
we must still love the bones,
carry them around with us in a burlap bag,
then brick them up in the walls of our new mansion,
in our new century,
so that, lest we forget, in our pride and arrogance,
we can put our ear close and hear
their tales of love and death—

And if something from the past must survive,
let it be Aquarius, water bearer,
who plants the seeds
and pours the warm sweet water from his jug

and tends the tender shoots that grow,
blind and dumb, inexorable and innocent,
ignorant of past and future, of all but their own growing.

Or if not Aquarius,
let it be my father, splayfooted,
shuffling down the humus-rich rows,
probing the earth with his thick long fingers,
watering with his huge gentleness,
demanding a wooden coffin so that his bones
would enrich the earth once more in death.
Born with the dying century, 1901,
he saw the first airplanes, radio, television;
new planets discovered, new stars;
new stars blooming over Hiroshima, Nagasaki, and
a mountain of bones in Auschwitz.
So much to hate in the old tired century,
which he loved,
because he was a great lover.
On January 22, 1966, his pills back in the house,
gulping the bright cold morning air,
he spread straw over the tender young strawberry plants
which, this spring, he knew, would bear.

If something from the past must survive,
let it be the memory of what was good,
of what we loved best.
Let it be Aquarius, let it be my father.

* * *

If you are born under this sign—an earth sign, a water sign—
you are blessed, you are remembered, the grass over your grave
is watered with our tears.

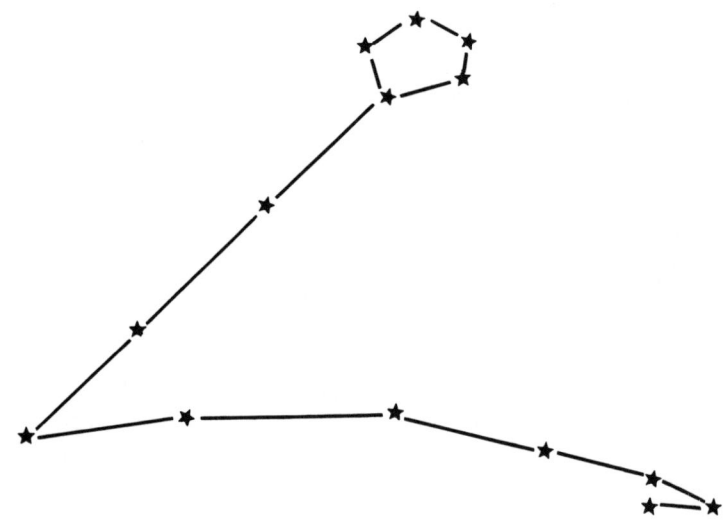

XII.
Challenger
(February 20-March 20)

Donny Smith, 10-B
English, Mrs. Wilkes
March 13, 1989

What the Challenger Disaster
Means to Me

My father says that the space shuttle Challenger disaster means the end of America. Basically I think he's right. In this essay I'm going to tell you why I think the Challenger disaster means the end of America. The Challenger disaster means the end of America for three reasons. First, it means the end of America because it shows that we can't do anything right anymore. Second, it means the end of America because nobody will take the blame for it. Third, it means the end of America because what goes up must come down. The first two reasons I basically got from my father, but the last one is all mine.

First, the Challenger disaster means the end of America because it's just one more in a long line of stuff that we can't do right. My father says that when he was a kid you could count on America succeeding at whatever it tried. We won World War I & II. The countries that we whipped in wars include England, Spain, Germany, Italy, Mexico, Austria, Japan, plus many others. But then they wouldn't let us fight to win in Korea, my father says (I wasn't born yet then so I can't say myself one way or another) which started us on the downhill that only got worse in Vietnam. It was like a swamp we couldn't get out of, my father says. We could have won Vietnam, my father says, but the politicians wouldn't let us. It was kind of like the refs taking a game away from you like they did us against the Russians in the Olympics. We'd never lost a game until then and now we can't win for losing. It's a shame and a disgrace. We can't build things right anymore either. My father says when he was a kid Made in Japan on something was a big joke, but now Made in the USA is a joke. So we shouldn't think of the Challenger disaster as any big surprise. It was pretty predictable, like my father says.

The second reason that the Challenger disaster means the end of America is that no one will take the blame for it. No one wants to take responsibility for their actions nowadays, my father says. Some politician gets caught with his hand in the cookie jar and he'll scream that he's been framed. Some nut shoots a couple dozen innocent people and he'll says it's not his fault because he grew up poor. Like when we took our Honda back to the used car place where we bought it because the clutch or something was bad and they wouldn't fix it even though we'd only had it a month. So sue us they said, which my father says is pretty typical of America these days. My father says if the Challenger disaster had happened in Japan, somebody would have opened a vein over it, and that's why Japan is taking over the world and we're second rate.

Third, last but not least, what goes up must come down. I mean, it seems to me that things just naturally peter out after awhile. Nothing lasts forever. You can't be on top forever. The Celtics looked like they couldn't be beat for awhile, then Larry Bird got hurt and now look at them. My dog Rosco lived old for a dog, fifteen years, but he died. What I'm getting at is, maybe America has just had its day, and like it or not it's time for somebody else to take over.

In conclusion, I have to admit that I'm not too sure what the whole thing means. All I know for a fact is that the ride down must have been a bad one. From what I've heard they were alive on the way down, which I can't hardly stand to think about. If they were here to tell us, they could tell us what it's like, what it all means, but of course they're not here. So maybe it doesn't mean the end of America. Then again, maybe it does.

* * *

An earth, air, fire, and water sign, the Challenger disaster occurred at T+74 seconds, January 28, 1986, at which point there was less than fifteen years left in the century. We plunge toward the end. Frantically, we claw at one another to free ourselves from the restraining harnesses—but to what purpose? There is no parachute to let us down gradually, and the craft has not been designed to withstand a sudden impact. We were caught off guard. We claw at one another. We scream.